EIGHT SECOND RIDE

THREE RIVERS RANCH ROMANCE: BOOK SEVEN

LIZ ISAACSON

AEJ CREATIVE WORKS

"The Lord is my strength and my shield; my heart trusted in him, and I am helped: therefore my heart greatly rejoiceth; and with my song will I praise him."

— PSALMS 28:7

The clothes Brynn Bowman wore had never weighed so much. Of course, she'd never chosen her saggiest jeans, her oldest cowgirl boots, or a canvas jacket that should've been retired years ago to meet anyone before.

But Tanner Wolf had insisted she make the six-hour drive to the small, Texas town of Three Rivers to pick him up and drive him out to some ranch. Some ranch where some cowhand worked. Some ranch Tanner believed held the key to his calf roping future.

She pulled into the gas station on the northern edge of town, her defenses on high as she coasted to a stop next to Tanner himself. She left the engine idling as she got out and stretched her back, already aware of the murderous winds and cool early-December temperatures.

Tanner scanned her like she carried a contagious disease. "I told you to wear something nice."

"I heard you," Brynn said as she studied the horizon, where a storm threatened. She pinned him with her most spiteful glare. "I just don't care about what you said."

His dark eyes turned hard as coal, a look he usually wore for someone else. She'd tried a relationship with Tanner a few years back, and that had ended almost before it began. Fun and fast, the broken relationship had left Brynn's fragile ego in pieces.

She'd been picking them up since, going out with a few men here and there, but each date seemed forced, with cowboys who could only talk about one thing: rodeo.

Brynn wanted someone, *anyone*, but a cowboy. Someone who could see she was more than a champion barrel racer. Someone who knew a woman had more to her than a title—if she could even get them to notice she was a woman at all.

Tanner sighed, the fight leaving his expression as he yanked open the passenger door of her truck. "I'm surprised this old beast made it down here."

She'd brought her father's truck, half-hoping it would break down on the Interstate somewhere in Southern Colorado. Then she wouldn't have to be Tanner's errand girl. Why she'd said she'd help him, she wasn't sure.

Oh, yes, she was. As she slid into the driver's seat and buckled up, she remembered why she'd driven almost four hundred miles. Whoever lived out at Three Rivers Ranch would be better than Tanner inviting her ex-fiancé to be his calf roping partner. She hadn't backed down in that argument, and her payment was to help Tanner find a suitable header who could train in time for the start of the rodeo season.

"You remember what to say?"

She snorted as she accelerated along the two-lane road. "You practically gave me a script. Say this. Don't say that." She lifted her hand and faced her palm toward him when he opened his mouth to speak. "I got it."

"I could just call Da—"

"Don't you dare," she hissed. "I'll get this guy to agree. What's his name again?"

"Ethan," Tanner said, his voice on the outer edge of frustration. "And I don't know how you're gonna convince anyone that joinin' the rodeo circuit is a good thing." He reached over and slid his finger down her leg like he could collect a bunch of dust from her faded jeans. "Ethan likes pretty women."

Great, she thought. *Another shallow cowboy.* Just what Brynn needed. She'd been raised by a single father who couldn't breathe if he wasn't in a stable, along with two older brothers who trained horses twenty-four/seven. Becoming a barrel racer had been in her blood, and she couldn't deny that any more than she could force herself to stop breathing.

But after her mama had died a decade ago, Brynn craved the company of someone who didn't wear a cowboy hat, didn't know which brand of boots were best for bull riding, didn't care who currently held the top spot for the Xtreme Bulls Riding Championship.

In her circles, someone like that didn't exist. As Brynn made the turn from highway to dirt road, she considered—again—quitting the rodeo altogether. She wondered what her father would say then.

She pulled into a nice parking lot in front of a newer building and swung her attention to Tanner. "Okay. So where is he?"

Tanner checked his watch like he didn't know what time it was. "He'll be in the horse barn. Invite him to dinner."

Annoyance flashed through Brynn with the speed of a flash flood. She contained it behind a poisonous smile. "You got it, boss."

"Don't call me—" She slammed the truck door, effectively silencing Tanner's words. The horse barn sat across the street to the north, and Brynn strode in that direction. Her pulse thrummed, though she did have Tanner's blasted script memorized.

The sun dipped lower in the sky as she walked, and she cursed winter. At least in Texas, there wasn't two feet of snow on the ground. A few seconds passed before her eyes adjusted to the dim interior of the barn. Someone moved at the far end, and she went that way, reaching her fingers out and petting the multiple horse noses that stretched over the fence to smell her.

The clothes she'd chosen definitely smelled like they belonged on a ranch. The cowboy heard her coming and turned in her direction. He tipped his hat with one hand while he kept a firm grip on the reins of a large black stallion with the other.

"What can I do for you?" he asked, his voice as soft as melting butter. Something vibrated inside her chest. What would her name sound like in his velvety voice?

He's a cowboy, she told herself sternly. *And probably about to become a bull rider.* Which, in Brynn's opinion, was ten times worse.

"I'm lookin' for Ethan Greene," she said.

The cowboy paused in his work completely. "You found 'im." He looked her up and down, his bright blue eyes arcing with lightning. His mouth settled into a tight line, his teeth obviously clenched. "Give me two seconds to put Lincoln away."

She wandered down the aisle as he spoke in a low tone and secured the gate on the horse's pen before joining her. In the waning light coming from the barn's entrance, Brynn found broad shoulders, a hint of blond hair under his cowboy hat, and very capable hands on Ethan.

"I'm Brynn, a friend of Tanner Wolf," she started.

"Oh, boy." Ethan stopped and swiped his hat off his head. "He sent out a pretty woman to try to convince me to be a calf roper?"

Warmth flowed through Brynn at his assessment of her looks. She tried to shake it away, tamp it down, but it didn't go far.

"Look," she said, glad her voice didn't sound too sweet, or too emotional, the way she felt. "I don't really care if it's you or someone else who becomes his header. It just can't be Da—" She clamped her lips shut. No way she was saying his name. She didn't want to explain about Dave Patton, not to this gorgeous stranger.

He peered at her, something alive and electric in his eyes as he tried to figure out how she might have finished that sentence. She stuck her hands in her pockets and lifted her chin. The end of her braid felt heavy against her chest; her boots squeezed against her toes. Why was this man's gaze undoing all her hard-fought years of cowboy resistance? What about him was so magnetic?

No matter what it was, it pulled against her. Pulled, and pulled, and pulled, until she unpocketed her hands and unstuck her voice. "It's a good gig," she said. "Tanner said you're the best rider he's seen in years. So you'll come train in Colorado Springs for a while. The pro circuit starts in February. If you can get a sponsor—and Tanner already has his lined up—then your travel and expenses are paid. It's not a bad life. Regular season ends in September, usually, but you can do the pro circuit; that goes all the way into December. And the purse is pretty great if you win. Tanner's looking to be a back-to-back champion in team roping." At least she'd stuck mostly to the script. "You can rope?"

Ethan swallowed and she watched the motion of his suntanned throat. "Did Tanner say I could?"

She shrugged. "I didn't get all the details."

A chuckle escaped his lips, drawing her attention there. The temperature in the barn skyrocketed to summer proportions, and Brynn darted her eyes away.

"Right," he drawled. "Because that didn't sound like a sales pitch for the PRCA or anything."

"Oh, so you know about the PRCA?"

His face darkened. "Used to be in it, cowgirl."

The word lashed her insides, eradicating all previous heat she'd felt toward Ethan. "Fine, whatever. I don't care if you're his partner or not." She finally got her legs to move toward the exit.

He matched her pace easily. "Sure you do. You just said it can be anyone but Da. Who's Da?"

"No one," she snapped.

"Why don't you like the PRCA?"

"Who said I didn't like it?" She stepped from the barn and the wind hit her like a punch to the nose. She flinched, but kept going.

"I have eyes," he said, still at her side.

Oh, she'd almost lost herself in the depth of those eyes. She determinedly didn't look at them again. Instead, she focused on Tanner, on the downward slide of his lips, on the way his shoulders lifted as if to say, *Well, is he coming to dinner?*

Dinner.

The word almost tripped her. "Hey," she said, turning back. "Are you done here on the ranch?"

Ethan looked over her shoulder, which wasn't hard as he stood a good eight inches taller than her. "Why? What'd you have in mind?" He took a step closer, something strange crossed his expression, and he fell back two paces.

"Dinner," she said. "I drove all the way from Colorado Springs today, and I haven't eaten since breakfast." She omitted the fact that her stomach had been rioting against her for days as she prepared for this trip.

Ethan glanced to where Tanner sat waiting in the cab of her truck. "Just me and you?"

Her gut flipped again, but this time because of the possibility of being alone with Ethan. "Sure." She put on her most charming smile, the one she usually reserved for her father and the reporters. "Just me and you."

ETHAN DIDN'T THINK HE'D EVER SHOWERED AS FAST AS HE DID after Brynn had said she'd go talk to Tanner and see if he could take her truck back to town so they could ride into Three Rivers together. He'd pointed her in the right direction to find his cabin, and said she could come on in when she was ready.

She wasn't in the cabin when he emerged from the back

bedroom, smelling like clean denim and his best, spicy cologne. His brain seemed to be battling with itself at a hundred miles an hour.

What are you doing?

Going to dinner.

You like her.

I do not. She invited me.

She's pretty.

So what?

But Ethan knew he couldn't go falling for another pretty woman. He'd asked out every available girl over the age of twenty-five in Three Rivers. Well, maybe not every single one. He'd gone on a few dates with the same woman several times, but the relationships always fizzled out. Half the time he got downright rejected when he asked, like Kelly Armstrong and Carly Winters had done.

He didn't want to repeat his past mistakes. He'd been working for a solid year on reinventing himself, thinking that perhaps if he didn't come at women with both guns blazing, he'd have better success.

And yet, old habits never seemed to die. The way he stepped closer to Brynn, all "What'd you have in mind?" made his muscles tighten and his face heat up. He wasn't going to take that approach, not with her.

Give me the words to say, he prayed as he moved through his cabin toward the front door. *Help me be the man a woman would actually want.*

The better part of his year had been spent soul-searching, first as he started going to church with Garth and his wife, Juliette. Then as he realized some of the mistakes he'd made in the past. Then as he started wanting to be the best person he could be. He still wasn't sure who that man was, but he wasn't giving up until he knew.

He pulled open the front door and found Brynn lying in the

hammock he'd installed last summer, fast asleep. He analyzed her features while he could. Long, dark hair she'd plaited into a single braid. Dark skin that came from hours in the sun, probably while in a saddle. He recognized the gait of another rider easily enough. Even during his own rodeo days, he knew who the bull riders were, who preferred bronc riding, and who did barrel racing.

He'd pegged her for barrel racing, something that suited her lithe frame and strong spirit really well.

As he stood there contemplating her offer—well, Tanner's offer—Ethan wondered if he could go back to the PRCA. He'd left because his girlfriend at the time didn't want to travel for six months out of the year, and she couldn't stand to be home alone while he was on the road.

He realized after he quit, and after Suzy left him, how paranoid she was. How insecure.

But he couldn't force himself to go back—too much pride for that. But this...this could be a way back into the PRCA where he didn't have to explain why he'd left. It had been six years, besides. No one would even recognize him.

At least he hoped not.

Ethan took a deep breath of the fresh, ranch air, and immediately regretted the idea of leaving this place. It had become home, even if he hadn't been able to find anyone to share it with. Even if he'd watched most of his friends find love and settle down, have families.

He still had time. He told himself that on a regular basis, and today was no different.

A door slammed, startling his heart into overdrive and waking Brynn. The hammock rustled, the chain squealed, and she flung her legs over the side.

"Sorry," she said, a delicious blush creeping from under her collar to kiss her cheeks.

Ethan cleared his throat to tame his thoughts. "It's fine. We don't have to go to dinner."

She peered up at him from under long lashes, her mocha eyes capturing his gaze and devouring it whole. "You're not hungry?"

"I'm hungry," he managed to say through a dry throat. "More thirsty, really."

"Hey, Ethan," Garth called from next door. "You wanna—?" He cut off as Brynn unfolded herself from the hammock. "Oh." Garth blinked like he'd never seen a woman before.

"I'm gonna head into town." Ethan hooked his thumb over his shoulder in the direction of Three Rivers. "Should I get that feed while I'm there? Save you the trip."

Garth leaned against his porch railing, his sharp foreman's gaze missing nothing, including the tiny shuffle-step Ethan took to put a teensy bit more distance between him and Brynn. "Sure, why not?

"Great," Ethan said. "Garth, this is Brynn...." He glanced at her, but she didn't offer him her last name. "A friend of a friend. Brynn, this is my boss, Garth. He's the foreman here at Three Rivers Ranch."

Garth nodded at her, and she man-nodded right back. A flicker of attraction flared to life deep in Ethan's core. He shouldn't be that impressed by her aloof behavior, but he found Brynn...intriguing.

And beautiful, the soft part of his brain added.

"Okay, let's go," Ethan said, wanting to grab onto her arm and take her down the steps with him. But she didn't exactly seem like the touchy-feely type. So he clomped down the stairs by himself, satisfied when she followed, caught up to him, and matched her stride to his.

HE MANAGED TO MAKE IT TO TOWN WITHOUT MAKING A FOOL OF

himself. Which, for Ethan, meant he didn't ask Brynn out for real or make any passes at her. A balloon filled with accomplishment swelled in his chest as he considered where to go for dinner.

"You like burgers?" he asked.

She wrinkled her nose. "Is there anywhere else?"

"You're in Texas." He glanced at her, sure she was joking. Who didn't like a hamburger?

She glared at him. "Anything like Thai? Or a salad bar. I could really use something smothered in ranch dressing right now."

Ethan refrained from rolling his eyes. "You know, you can have them put ranch dressing on a burger." He turned left so he wouldn't have to look at her, and headed for the all-you-can-eat buffet. They'd have rabbit food—and steak.

He pulled into the parking lot, but Brynn protested. "I can't eat here."

Ethan stopped his truck and full-on scanned her like he could find defects just by looking. "Why not?"

"Too many germs." She shuddered.

"Good gravy," he mumbled under his breath. "Why don't you figure out where you want to go?" He didn't mean the words to come out with such an acidic bite, especially because his tone made Brynn's coffee-colored eyes frost over.

"I don't know anywhere here."

"How about I drive around and you tell me when you see something that looks satisfactory?"

He thought she'd like that, but her frown deepened and her fists clenched. "I don't need to be catered to." She reached for the door. "This is fine."

Ethan punched the lock before she could grip the door handle. "This is not fine. You said you didn't like buffets."

"I can cope."

"You don't need to. There's lots of places to eat. Maybe not Thai...."

She flexed her fingers and curled them tighter. Flex, curl. "Why do you care?"

"*You* asked *me* to dinner. I'm just trying to be nice."

"I don't need you to be nice."

Ethan sighed. Even when he tried a different tactic, he couldn't win. "Look," he said. "Let's just start over." He reached for his phone, which he'd tossed on the dashboard when he'd left the ranch. "How about I map some places and you let me know if they sound good?" He didn't wait for her to respond. "Okay, great." He opened his map app, and typed in "nearby restaurants."

"All right, cowgirl, we've got—" He cut off at the sound of a growl coming from her throat. He glanced at her, impressed by how fast she could lock her jaw. "Okay, sorry." He cleared his throat, wishing her anger didn't make him want to call her cowgirl again, see if maybe she'd touch him, even if it was to slug him in the shoulder for being chauvinistic.

"Oh, look, Thai Pan." He tilted the phone toward her. "Never been there. Can't say if it's good or not." He suspected it wouldn't be. Seriously, who came to the Texas Panhandle and wanted to eat Thai food?

He put his truck in gear when she didn't argue and headed toward the western edge of town, where Thai Pan waited. With each passing moment, he wondered how Brynn had roped him into this dinner, into considering going back to the rodeo, into eating food with names he couldn't even pronounce.

Brynn's blood boiled as Ethan pulled into the Thai place. She didn't even know why she'd argued with him. He *was* trying to be nice, and she should've just accepted that.

Why couldn't she accept that?

"You comin'?" he asked as he leaned back into the cab. "Or do you suddenly feel like Italian?"

Again, her ire bristled against his playful tone. She wanted to curse Tanner up one side and down the other. He was probably relaxing in his hotel room, feet up, and the meal of his choice from room service at his side.

Her stomach roared, successfully reminding her that she needed Ethan to at least consider being Tanner's header. She would not, could not, face Dave again in this lifetime.

"Of course," she bit out as she released her seatbelt.

Ethan cast her a curious glance as she neared him at the front of the truck. Her insides turned soft and gooey, and she told herself to be nice. It certainly wasn't his fault she was here. She didn't need to take out her temper on the innocent cowboy.

Or maybe she did. She disliked all cowboys as a general rule.

Maybe it's time to break one of your rules, she thought, stumbling as the idea took root in her mind and began to grow.

The restaurant wasn't busy, and they got a table as soon as they walked through the door. Ethan sipped his water, made a face, and focused on her. "So," he said. "You live in Colorado Springs?"

"Yeah," she said, lifting her own water glass to her lips. She took the tiniest of sips, and detected the distinct flavor of rose petals. She licked her lips like that would rid her mouth of the disgusting taste. "I lived in Dallas until I was fifteen, though." She threw him half a smile. "Too many burgers. Had to move."

Ethan returned the grin in full force, causing Brynn's heart to trip over its beat. The waiter returned, and she asked for a couple of lemon wedges, hoping for extra time to get her pulse under control.

"Make that a couple dozen," Ethan said, eyeing the water like it had turned to tar. "And I have no idea what to order." He looked at her with a hopeful expression, and with those glorious blue eyes drinking her in, her frustration fell down another notch.

She coached him through the menu and added as much lemon juice to her water as she thought she could stand. It still tasted disgusting, and she pushed it away as the waiter returned with their shrimp and mango spring rolls. As she took a bite, she couldn't think of a single thing to say, opening the door for Ethan to ask questions. Questions she wouldn't want to answer.

He led with, "So why'd you really move to Colorado Springs?"

"My dad and brothers wanted to get more involved in the rodeo after Mama died."

"Oh, I'm sorry." Sadness paraded through his expression.

She waved her hand like her mother's absence didn't bother her. "Happened a long time ago."

"How long?"

"Ten years. I was fifteen."

Ethan cocked his head, his eyes thoughtful. Brynn thought she could dive into them and find perfectly warm ocean water.

"My mom lives in Littleton," he said. "I don't get to see her much."

"Siblings?"

"Nope." He leaned back as the waiter arrived with his Thai beef salad and her Pad Thai.

She deftly changed the conversation topic back to the rodeo, but she hadn't taken two bites before she realized she'd just done what she hated most about the men she'd dated.

Could she only talk about the rodeo circuit? Who was sitting at the top of the leader boards, who'd hurt himself during last night's bull ride, who had mentioned retiring, even in passing?

She gave herself a little shake, reminding herself that Tanner hadn't paid her gas money and a night in a hotel for her to get to know Ethan Greene. She *needed* to talk rodeo with him so he'd become Tanner's header.

Nothing more, she told herself sternly even as she admired the puzzled look on his face as he took a taste of his beef.

"There's something wrong with this," he said, reaching for the disgusting water.

"It's Thai," she said.

"It tastes rotten."

She couldn't help laughing, couldn't help the twitch of magnetism that brought her closer to Ethan when he returned her smile, couldn't help noticing his strong jaw and taut muscles as he replaced the water glass and folded his arms across his chest without taking another bite.

"I think you'll really like the rodeo circuit," she said. "Why'd you leave the first time?"

Storm clouds rolled through his eyes, turning their delightfully blue color into shades of gray. "Why don't you like being a champion barrel racer?"

Her throat closed. "How did you know I'm a—?" She waved her empty fork, her appetite gone. "A barrel racer?"

"A *champion* barrel racer." He tapped his phone, which lay face-down on the table. "I have a data plan. Your name brings up scads of articles."

"When did you even look?"

"While you squeezed two whole lemons into your water to make it taste better."

Brynn lifted her chin, her automatic defense mechanism. How could this man make her go from hot to cold in under two seconds? "I don't remember telling anyone I didn't like barrel racing."

"Yeah, I didn't see that online," he said. "But I can see it in your face, cowgirl. I'm really good at reading people."

"I'm—" She cut herself off, unsure of how to finish. "I'm tired," she finally said, going with the truth.

Surprise flickered across his face. "Tired of what? Winning?"

Her shoulders sagged, and she tossed a prayer heavenward that she could make it through this night, this dinner, this conversation. "Everything."

THE VULNERABILITY WITH WHICH BRYNN SPOKE TUGGED AGAINST Ethan's heart, no matter how much he wished it wouldn't. "I feel like that sometimes," he said, a shocked thrill running through him. He didn't confess to being tired, ever. He was Ethan Greene, the general controller and hardest working cowhand Three Rivers had. Nothing scared him. Nothing made him waver.

Nothing but the woman seated across the table from him. Her chin wobbled the tiniest bit, and Ethan wanted to scoop her up and assure her everything would be fine. She could quit barrel racing if she wanted to. Move anywhere in the country. Do anything.

He looked away instead, signaling the waiter to bring the check. He'd drop Brynn off at her hotel, get her number like he was really considering rejoining the rodeo circuit, and then stop by a drive-through for something edible.

He wasn't in a huge hurry to get back to his empty, dark cabin, but he didn't know how to deal with distressed women.

Silence descended on them while they waited for his card to process, while they walked back to his truck. He opened her door for her, blocking her way with one arm as she tried to pass. "If you want to quit, why don't you?"

Her soft eyes tightened and she shrugged. He got the message: None of his business.

And it really wasn't. He barely knew her—reading a couple of Internet articles didn't count. Neither did his super-detective observation skills.

Ethan couldn't think of anything to say, except things the old Ethan would say, and he kept his mouth shut as she navigated him to a hotel in the center of town.

"So I should probably get your number," he said, his voice coming out lower than normal.

"You should?" She swung toward him. "Why?"

Embarrassment swept through him and he pulled his hat down over his eyes. "Never mind. I guess I can call Tanner and let him know I'm not going to be his header."

She cocked her head to the side, as if trying to understand his words. "Why don't you want to be his header? He already has sponsors. All you'd need to do is get yourself to Colorado Springs by the new year."

Ethan couldn't explain why he didn't want to be Tanner's header, wasn't exactly sure why. "He should've come and talked to me himself."

"He said he tried." Her voice dropped in volume.

"Not that hard." He'd come out to the ranch once, way back at the beginning of August. Months had passed since then, and

Ethan hadn't heard from him. Then he'd sent a pretty woman, knowing about Ethan's past. A past he'd worked hard to overcome. A past he didn't want to repeat.

"Are you the same person you were last year?" he asked, not quite sure why the question came out of his mouth.

Brynn exhaled and shifted on the seat. "I don't know. Maybe."

"I'm not," he said, finally lifting his gaze to meet hers. "And that's why I don't want to be Tanner's header."

Her lips turned down in disapproval. She held out her hand.

"What?" he asked.

"Give me your phone. I'll put in my number. That way, when you change your mind, you can call me and buy me a decent dinner."

A smile tugged against Ethan's mouth, against his resolve. "Hey, you picked Thai, not me." He handed her his cell.

"Tanner's going to pay for my room service," she said as she tapped on his phone. "I'll bill him for whatever you get now that you've dropped me off."

"I wasn't—" Ethan laughed. "Okay, I totally was gonna go through a drive-through. I can't get that disgusting floral taste out of my mouth."

She giggled with him and extended his phone toward him. "Okay, Ethan." She didn't release the phone when he gripped it; his fingers tingled as they wrapped around hers. "Seriously. Call me when you change your mind."

"You're awfully confident I'm gonna change my mind."

She released the phone and slid her fingers away from his. He felt the loss deeper than was possible. He didn't understand why. Brynn wasn't particularly nice to him, though she did have some vulnerable moments. He ached to get to know the woman underneath the angry exterior. Maybe he should change his mind about the rodeo circuit....

She opened the door and slid into the night. Before she closed the door, she said, "Maybe I want to see you again."

The door slammed, leaving Ethan with the ghost of her words haunting his ears. Light from the hotel illuminated her, and he waited until she entered the building, never once looking back.

"She doesn't want to see you again," he muttered to himself as he swung his truck toward the nearest fast food joint.

Did she?

ETHAN ROSE BEFORE THE SUN THE NEXT MORNING—SOMETHING easy to do in the winter. Still, he'd barely slept the night before, or at least his mind felt that way. He'd obsessed over Brynn well into the wee morning hours before finally succumbing to exhaustion. And now he had a full schedule of ranch work on the horizon.

He rode his black stallion, Lincoln, out to the bullpens to toss out a fresh batch of hay and issue clean water. He'd always been drawn to the large animals, and he took an extra moment to lean against the fence and watch the black bulls go after the food.

Maybe he should take Tanner's offer. He'd been a fairly decent roper in the past, though his twenty-year-old self wouldn't let him compete in team roping. Back then, his pride dictated that he be a champion bull rider. Nothing else would do.

Now, a bit older and marginally wiser, Ethan wondered if he could rope *and* ride bulls. He issued a shrill whistle, and the smallest bull glanced up, but went back to the hay before Ethan could blink.

"Ethan!" someone called.

Ethan turned toward the voice and found Aaron atop a mahogany horse with white splotches. Patches. Ethan worked with Aaron often, usually on remote assignments as neither of them had someone who needed them back at the ranch.

A frown pulled at Ethan's mouth. He didn't have anyone who needed him, period. The distant thought that he should call his mother crossed his mind, but he silenced it easily as Aaron trotted up the fence line.

"What's up?" Ethan asked, his mind churning about the rodeo. If he joined, he'd be closer to his mom. And Tanner would need him....

"Boss wants you to check the herd in section four before lunch. Then there's a fence in the calving arena one of the pregnant heifers kicked through. He wants you to take a truck out there this afternoon. And then he wants you to plan the staff meeting for tomorrow mornin'."

Ethan waited patiently, though the list of tasks weighed on him like a hundred-pound sack of oats.

"And one of the tractors won't start," Aaron continued. "He wants me on that, but he wants you to come check on me before you finish for the day."

Ethan lifted his hat and scrubbed his fingers through his hair. "I set myself to check the herd in section six," he said. "Garth wants me to do all that other stuff?"

Aaron blinked, clearly unsure what to do.

"I'll do that too," Ethan said, the restless night drawing his tone into one of resignation.

"Great." Aaron flashed him a smile and turned Patches back in the direction of the ranch. "I'll tell Garth."

Ethan took another minute to watch him go, then he swung back onto Lincoln and headed out on the open range to check on the cattle.

As Lincoln trotted along, Ethan couldn't get the endless questions out of his mind. After a while, he decided to do something he'd recently learned to do: pray.

He closed his eyes, trusting his horse to know the way, and took a deep breath. The air smelled like wind and rain, and Ethan wasn't sure he could leave Three Rivers Ranch.

Lord, I love it here, but could I feel the same way in Colorado Springs? Should I be Tanner's header?

The breeze picked up, threatening to unseat Ethan's cowboy hat. He pressed one hand to his head at the same time the wind morphed into the words, *You could be happy in Colorado.*

His stomach fell to his boots with the answer he didn't want.

But if God was going to spare a few moments to let him know what to do, Ethan thought he should at least try to listen.

3

Brynn woke to the sound of her phone buzzing against her nightstand. Her alarm hadn't gone off yet, which meant her caller was a morning person.

She groaned as she rolled over and pawed for her phone. She found it and squinted one eye to swipe on the call.

"Yeah?"

"Brynn?"

The voice coming through the line stirred something inside Brynn, but she couldn't quite place what. "Yeah. Who's this?"

"Ethan Greene." He let his name hang there, and while it did, Brynn's traitorous heart pounded harder than she liked.

"Go on." She pulled herself into a seated position, wondering if he'd thought about her parting words to him as often as she had over the past three days.

"I've decided to give your offer a shot."

"It's not *my* offer," she said. "Tanner—"

"Yeah, yeah," Ethan said. "When's the latest you need me in Colorado Springs?"

"*I* don't need you—"

"Did you or did you not say you wanted to see me again?" The playful nature of his question sent a shot of honey through her insides.

She had said that. She'd hoped he hadn't heard. Or maybe she'd wanted him to. She wasn't sure.

"You still there, cowgirl?"

With that word, the honey turned to sludge. "I'm sure you have Tanner's number. *He'll* give you all the details you need."

"Okay, truce," Ethan said. "You said I could call you."

"And you have."

He exhaled, but it didn't sound angry. Brynn cocked her head to the side, trying to capture every minute sound through the phone.

"I was hoping...."

She gave him a few seconds to finish, but when he remained mute, she asked, "Hoping for what?"

"Hoping for some help up there. You know, finding a place to live, getting an inside scoop on who's who in the rodeo, that kind of thing."

Brynn instantly wanted to help him. Show him around Colorado Springs, eat lunch with him, watch the laugh lines around his eyes crinkle as they bantered. Still, something inside her stopped her from accepting right away. Probably his voice calling her *cowgirl*.

"Doesn't your mom live near here? She can help you find an apartment."

Nothing came through the line. "You still there, cowboy?"

A low growl entered her ear, followed by a hearty laugh. By the time he quieted, Brynn's internal temperature had risen at least ten degrees.

"Why don't you like being a cowgirl?" he asked, chasing all the heat from her system.

Her mind raced, searching for a response. Her throat stuck together and she needed a drink the way fish needed water. She finally came up with, "When do you think you'll be moving up here?"

"I'm not sure." A smile infused his voice. "I need to talk to my boss here. I can't leave him high and dry. Should I call Tanner to find out when he needs me there?"

"Nah," she said. "He'll start training at the same time as me. Just after the new year."

"Three weeks," Ethan murmured. "I can probably do that."

Brynn thought Ethan could probably do a lot, and her fantasies ran wild for a few seconds. She reined them in when he said, "Okay, great. I'll call you later when I know for sure."

She couldn't wait, but she was smart enough to keep that thought to herself this time. "Great," she said instead.

After he hung up, Brynn let a slow smile spread her lips. At the same time, she'd need to eventually answer his question about why she didn't want to be a cowgirl.

If only she knew the answer.

"Morning, Daddy." Brynn tipped up onto her toes to give her father a quick kiss on the cheek. He stood at the stove, his permanent cowboy hat already in place.

"Mornin'," he said, glancing away from the scrambled eggs he made every single morning. If there was one thing about Brynn's father she could count on, it was a hot breakfast. Followed by a morning horseback ride.

She switched on the radio that sat on the kitchen counter, the low sound of country music filling the space between them. "Where's Chuck?"

"Already in the barn," her dad said. "You should be out there too, lazybones."

"I got home really late," Brynn said. "And I never get out to the barn until at least ten anyway."

Her dad chuckled, turned off the burner, and scooped the eggs into a bowl. "How was the trip to Texas? Where'd you go again?"

"Three Rivers," she said, thinking of the quaint town, the peace that infused the ranch, Ethan. She startled when he entered her mind so easily, like he belonged there. He had looked at her differently than the cowboys here, but she suspected his interest would fade quickly once he started training with Tanner.

The man was relentless, demanding—and usually getting— perfection. *It's no wonder we didn't work out*, Brynn thought.

"And?" her dad prompted, bringing Brynn away from the edge of the self-conscious abyss she'd almost fallen into.

"And I talked to some cowboy about joining Tanner's roping team." She picked up a fork and speared some scrambled eggs. "He's thinking about it."

Her dad nodded as he added even more pepper to his eggs. Brynn didn't know how he could eat them like that. She thought the little he'd put in while they cooked was almost intolerable.

"What about you?" her dad asked. "When you startin' your training?"

Brynn's appetite evaporated. "Same as always, Daddy. Coupla weeks."

"You could get a head start," he said as Duke entered the kitchen. Her older brother wore jeans, his cowboy boots, and a blue flannel shirt. Oh, and his cowboy hat. Brynn wondered if he slept with it on. She'd crept into his room one night many years ago and discovered Duke had light brown hair.

"Hey," he said, reaching for his heavy, canvas jacket—much like the one she'd worn in Texas. Here in Colorado, it would provide protection against the winter weather, while she'd used hers as protection against a handsome cowboy.

You didn't know he was going to be handsome, she chided herself.

But he was, the irrational side of her brain countered.

He was all right.

Um, he looked way better than all right. And he has a sense of humor.

"Brynn?"

"Hmm?" She turned off her mental argument to focus on Duke.

"You comin'?"

Her temper flared, and she practically threw her fork to the counter. "What is it with you guys? I never go out to the barn this early."

Duke blinked a couple of times. "We got a new horse." He said it like, *Duh. Of course we'll be spending all day in the barn, starting as early as possible.*

Her father rose and shrugged into his jacket too. Brynn folded her arms. "You guys go on without me. I still haven't showered."

Neither of them seemed to notice the frost in her tone or the angry set of her mouth. And why should they? They had a new horse!

They left Brynn fuming in the kitchen. Would they ever see her as anything more than a cowgirl? Would anyone?

Once again, her thoughts turned to Ethan. She'd basked in his laugh, and while she appreciated the bulk of his muscles and the lines of his face, she'd also felt something teeming just behind his clear, blue eyes. Something she wanted to discover.

She pushed herself away from the table. "Don't be ridiculous," she mumbled. "He's a cowboy, and he's just like every other one out there."

By the time she joined her father and brothers in the barn, she'd managed to push Ethan Greene from her thoughts, hopefully for a good long while.

———

"WELL, I GUESS THAT'S IT." ETHAN HELD OUT THE KEY TO HIS

cowboy cabin. His cowboy cabin that he'd lived in for almost five years. Five years that had been the best of his life.

A sense of sadness overtook him, and just like everyday for the past three weeks, he wondered if he was doing the right thing. He'd talked to Garth about it at length. Pete Marshall too— because he wasn't just leaving Three Rivers Ranch, he was leaving behind the therapeutic riding program at Courage Reins too. His friends. The life he'd known for half a decade.

And for what? he wondered for at least the hundredth time.

Every time he made it to this part of the argument, God reminded him that he could be happy in Colorado. And while Ethan wasn't *un*happy in Three Rivers, he wasn't exactly fulfilled either.

"Yep," Garth said. "Drive safe. Say hello to your ma for me." He slid his arm around his wife, Juliette, who wore her emotion over Ethan leaving for all to see.

"I can't believe you're leaving." She seized Ethan and embraced him. "I'll miss you living right next door."

Ethan hugged her back, the bulk of her pregnant belly between them. "I'll miss you too, ma'am."

A small sob choked her laughter. "Oh, stop it. Go on, now." She released him and swatted him on the shoulder.

"If the baby is a boy," he said. "Ethan's a mighty fine name."

Juliette grinned—the reaction Ethan had hoped for. He didn't do well with weepy women, and Brynn entered his mind. She didn't seem like the crying type.

Or the cowboy type, he thought, and his lips turned down into a frown. She hadn't rejected his proposition of helping him, but she hadn't accepted it either.

"I best be goin'," he said. "It's almost six hours to Colorado, and I told my mom I'd be there for lunch."

Garth nodded, and Juliette hugged him again, and Ethan climbed into his pickup. He'd often wished he had a dog like Garth, but he'd never gotten around to getting one. He vowed as he headed down the rutted road toward the highway that he'd get one in Colorado.

He turned on the radio and cranked the volume. If he had to drive six hours alone, he could at least do it without thinking.

With the help of his smart phone, he pulled into his mother's split-level a few minutes after noon. Apprehension flowed from the soles of his boots to the top of his head. He hadn't seen his mom in person for years. Since he quit the rodeo and tried to find something else to do in Colorado Springs. He'd lived with her while he attempted to figure things out. In the end, he'd gone back to what called to him: being a cowboy.

His mother hadn't been happy about the move to Texas, but she preferred it over the bull riding. Ethan knew ranching was an around-the-clock job, and he'd kept in contact with his mom through social media and texts.

He took a deep breath and pushed his cowboy hat lower on his forehead. "Now or never," he muttered as his mom's figure appeared in the doorway. He headed up the front walk and took the few steps in two long strides.

"Mom." He opened the screen door and engulfed his petite mother in a hug. "It's good to see you." And he meant it. Years of unsaid words and missing embraces hung over him and he pressed his eyes closed.

"Ethan." Her voice reminded him of home, and a burst of gratitude spiraled through him. "The drive went okay?" She released him and stepped back into the house. "Come in, come in. It's going to snow this afternoon."

He moved into the house and she sealed the winter weather out.

"Upstairs, upstairs," she said, waving to the left. "Lunch should be coming out of the oven any minute."

As Ethan climbed the short stack of steps, he realized he should've stopped for lunch before showing up at his mother's.

He'd forgotten a lot about his childhood, but the burnt dinners and over-salted meats had stayed well-anchored in his memory.

"Smells good," he said, again speaking the truth. Something saucy and cheesy.

She slid on oven mitts and removed a large pan from the oven. Sure enough, tomato sauce bubbled around a crust of mozzarella cheese. "I've been taking cooking classes," she said. "This is about the hundredth lasagna I've made."

She stood back and watched him. He finally realized she was waiting for him to speak. "Looks great, Ma. I'm starving." He slid onto a barstool and basked in the warmth of her beaming smile. "How long you been cookin'?"

"A few years now. I usually take the food to my neighbors." She turned her back on him and sliced into the lasagna. "No one here to feed."

The barb jabbed Ethan in the fleshy part of his heart. But he didn't respond. They'd never had a productive conversation when he challenged one of her digs. With the force of a hurricane, he remembered why he'd left Colorado.

"How are things at the senior center?" he asked.

The spatula she used to lift the food from the pan got tossed into the sink. "I stopped going a few years ago."

Ethan sensed a storm brewing, but he couldn't think of anything else to ask her. "Why?"

"Oh, you know."

He picked up his fork. "No, Ma. I don't know." She'd never said anything about the senior center that he could remember. In fact, the crocheted potholders she'd sent him last week for Christmas testified that she still attended.

"They changed their programs. I didn't like it."

The lasagna tasted like magic in Ethan's mouth. "You must still find time to do your crafts."

"Of course."

"So what'd they change?" Ethan honestly didn't know why he

cared. Maybe because this was his mom and he wanted her to be happy.

"We got a new director, and he thought we needed more social activities."

Ethan quirked a smile. "You mean you had to talk to people? That's just terrible." He chuckled at the dark look on her face.

"I have my friends," she said. "I didn't need any more. Certainly not from *him*."

"Oh, *him*?" Ethan asked, his previous joviality gone. "He *liked* you?"

"I liked him too." She stuffed her mouth with a large bite of lasagna.

Ethan watched her face redden. "Mom, are you telling me you had a boyfriend and it didn't work out so you stopped going to the senior center?"

She swallowed. "Isn't that why you left Colorado? A bad breakup? At least I stayed in town."

Her words bit deep, and Ethan finished his lasagna and put his plate in the dishwasher. "Okay, well, I'm gonna go grab my bag. I've got three apartment showings lined up for tomorrow. I shouldn't be in your hair long."

He'd reached the front door when she called, "You can stay as long as you want, sweetie."

He lifted his hand in a wave, but he wouldn't be staying with his mother longer than necessary. Even a few days felt too long. He was twenty-seven-years-old, for crying out loud.

With his bag in his hand, he turned to go back to the house when his phone rang. Though the winter breeze threatened frostbite in only a few minutes, he swiped on the call from Brynn and stayed near the truck.

"Hey, Brynn," he said.

"Ethan." His name in her voice staved off the chill of the weather, though he wasn't sure what she possessed that drew him to her so immediately. "You make it to town?"

"Just got in," he said. "Had lunch with my mother."

A pause on the other end of the line reminded Ethan that Brynn couldn't have lunch with her mom.

He opened his mouth to apologize when she said, "That's nice."

"It wasn't that nice," Ethan said. "I'll tell you about it later. Want to go to dinner tonight?" He clamped his lips around the last word. "I mean, me and Tanner are gettin' together tonight, and you're welcome to come."

Ethen pressed his eyes closed and tilted his head toward the threatening sky. Why did he always jump to inviting women out? *Slow*, he coached himself.

"I'm sure I'll be in the way," she said. "I was just checkin' to make sure you'd made it."

"I made it," he managed to say.

"Great."

"Okay."

Again, the silence between them felt electric, like if the airwaves could speak they'd be able to say what Brynn and Ethan couldn't.

"Well, goodbye," Ethan said. Brynn repeated it and the call ended. Ethan fisted the phone in his hand, not sure why his tongue got so tied when it came to Brynn. Maybe he was fighting against who he really was. Maybe his nature was to charge full-steam ahead when it came to women, and he'd just have to keep doing it until he found one his forward nature didn't turn off.

Everything about such thoughts felt wrong, and Ethan went to his mother's guest bedroom with a strengthened resolve to keep his dinner invitations to himself.

4

"You will not call Luke and find out where Tanner's going to dinner." Brynn's jaw clenched as she paced in the tack room. "Don't do it. Do *not* do it." She spun and caught sight of her dad in the doorway.

"Workin' through something, baby?"

"I guess."

"Washington looked good today."

Brynn's mind lingered as far from her horse as possible. "Yeah," she said, trying to focus on the tight turns Washington had accomplished. "He'll be ready." Training didn't officially start until Monday, and Brynn planned on taking the next four days off before she'd be expected to live and breathe barrel racing.

"Well, I can see your mind's somewhere else." His bootsteps faded before Brynn realized he'd left.

She needed to pull herself together before she went to the house for dinner. Chuck would see something on her face and pester her relentlessly until the truth exploded from her. Her oldest brother, Chuck had taken on the role of her mother after Mama's death. Said someone had to ask the hard questions and learn the truth. She loved him for it as much as she hated his questions.

"Brynn!" Chuck's voice seemed to echo through the barn, finding Brynn in the tack room and reminding her that she wasn't forgotten. She loved her family, she did. Her brothers had always watched out for her, especially when they'd moved to Colorado Springs and she'd been hit on by every cowboy on the rodeo circuit. They'd get between her and whatever bronc rider had swaggered too close and remind him that she was only fifteen.

Soon enough, all the guys started seeing Brynn as one of them. Chuck hadn't had to threaten anyone in years, and Brynn hadn't been able to make it past a third date in just as long.

"Brynn!" Chuck called again. "Where are you?"

"Tack room," she said over her shoulder, taking a deep breath before she had to face him.

"There you are."

She turned toward Chuck. "Here I am. What're you blustering about?"

He sent her a lazy grin, a teasing sparkle in his dark eyes. She took after him—ebony hair, olive skin, chocolatey eyes. They both looked like their mother, and a stab of missing went through Brynn's core. Amazing, after a decade of her being gone that Brynn could still feel her absence so keenly.

"Tanner's at the house, askin' about you." Chuck hooked his thumb in the general direction of the house.

Brynn's heart banged against her ribs and then settled near her stomach. "Tanner?"

"Said he wants to see you for a second." Chuck's expression sobered. "He's not...you know. You guys aren't...."

Brynn crossed her arms and rolled her eyes. "Give me some credit." She stepped past him and strode down the aisle toward the barn's exit.

"I didn't think so," Chuck said, catching her. "I was just checkin'."

The wind slapped Brynn as she stepped into it. She tread the well-worn path in the snow, careful on the slickest parts. Chuck followed, another apology floating from his mouth.

"It's fine, Chuck. I'm just not into cowboys. You should know that."

"That's what you keep tellin' me."

"Then stop badgering me about it." She headed up the stairs to the deck, which led to the kitchen.

"I just don't see you datin' anyone."

She spun, only steps from entering the house. "So what?"

Chuck wore those concerned lines around his eyes that made Brynn's anger soften. "I just want you to be happy."

Brynn's chest tightened. Tightened against the words threatening to burst from her mouth. She couldn't say, *I'm going to quit barrel racing.*

Or *Maybe I want to try beauty school.*

Or *I'm moving across the country and living in the biggest city I can find.*

Truth was, all of those were things she'd rather do than start another PRCA season. Than defend her championship. Than spend another minute in Colorado Springs.

"You okay?" Chuck put his fingers under her chin and lifted her eyes to meet his.

She shook her head, still not able to trust herself to speak. Turning away, she pushed the traitorous words from her thoughts, expelled the pent-up air she'd been holding in her lungs, went to see what the devil Tanner wanted with her when he should be eating dinner with Ethan.

ETHAN'S INSIDES FELT STICKY AT THE SAME TIME THEY SEEMED coated in ice. Brynn's words—*I'm just not into cowboys*—looped in his mind, an endless, repeating cycle that left him feeling sicker and sicker by the minute.

He wasn't even sure why he cared. He'd spent maybe two hours with the woman—though she *had* taken up countless hours of thought over the past few weeks. He barely knew her, but this unnamed force inside him wanted to learn everything about her—including why she didn't like cowboys and if he could possibly persuade her otherwise.

He turned away from the barn he'd watched her march out of, turned back into the bitter night wind, turned his desire for Brynn as low as he could make it go. He wasn't here to find a girl-friend, that was for sure. He wasn't sure why Tanner had insisted they come to Brynn's before heading to dinner, and after he'd sat in the truck for ten minutes, Ethan had decided to walk around a bit. He couldn't help it if the sidewalk bordered her property. Couldn't help that he'd frozen on the spot when he saw her exit the barn. Couldn't help that he'd been cast in shadows and she hadn't seen him while she spoke to her brother.

At least Ethan hoped the man she'd been with was her brother. They seemed friendly, but not romantic.

Definitely a brother, he told himself as he slid into Tanner's still-idling truck. A few minutes later, Tanner came out of the house and ambled toward the driver's door.

"Ready?" he asked as he climbed in.

"Waitin' on you." Curiosity burned through Ethan's veins, but he wouldn't ask about Tanner's business with Brynn. He wouldn't talk about Brynn at all—Tanner would rib him mercilessly if Ethan let on that he liked her for more than some cowgirl on the rodeo circuit. Ethan himself couldn't even believe he liked her more than that already.

But again, something about her spoke intrigue to Ethan's soul. He had to know more about her.

"She had some keys I needed," Tanner said by way of expla-nation as he backed into the street.

Ethan managed to grunt as he kept his gaze focused out the passenger window. He didn't need to know *why* Brynn had keys Tanner needed. Didn't care.

He fed himself these lies as they drove to a steakhouse and settled into a booth. Tanner talked and waved his knife and fork and ordered dessert Ethan was too full to eat. He listened to the training schedule, promised to watch the championship roping segment Tanner had sent him, and confirmed that he'd be at the practice facility on Monday morning at eight a.m.

That schedule gave him four days to find an apartment. Four days to get moved in and somewhat settled. Four days to convince Brynn to give him the scoop on happenings inside the rodeo.

His fingers itched to text her, but he kept his phone in his back pocket while Tanner outlined what their days would look like. Roping practice all morning. Training with the horses after lunch, and then practice rounds with calves before heading over to the bullpens for a few lessons on bull riding.

After a few weeks of that, they'd switch to riding the mechanical bulls and taking balance classes. Soon after that, they'd head to San Antonio for their first rodeo, with dozens more to follow for the next twelve months. Weariness engulfed Ethan just thinking about it.

As Tanner dug into the chocolate brownie supreme— complete with caramel sauce—Ethan closed his eyes. *Lord, is roping and bull riding really going to make me happy?*

God stayed silent on the issue, leaving Ethan more unsettled than ever.

THE NEXT MORNING FOUND ETHAN IN BRYNN'S NECK OF THE WOODS again. Stupid hope flowed through him that he'd accidentally bump into her, that they could talk for a few minutes. But her house seemed as dormant as every other one on the block as

Ethan crawled by in his pickup. He turned the corner and continued halfway down the block to the address he'd typed into his phone.

It wasn't an apartment building like he'd been expecting, but a single-family home. He'd arrived a couple of minutes early, and he wasn't going to get out when the temperatures made his breath billow in clouds around his face.

Right at nine o'clock, a car pulled in behind him. A tall, lean man got out and Ethan joined him on the sidewalk. "Miles Yancey?"

"You must be Ethan Greene." The realtor grinned like Ethan was the President of the United States. "Welcome to Colorado Springs."

Ethan allowed himself to return the smile and shake the man's hand. "I thought we were lookin' at apartments."

"Oh, this is a rental," Miles assured him. "The woman who lives here rents out her back cottage."

Cottage sounded like something elderly women in England lived in, but Ethan followed Miles down the driveway, past the quaint, single-story home, and into the backyard.

Miles pointed to the garage. "That's for you. Mrs. Barkley parks in the one on the other side of the house. She maintains the backyard and garden, so I hope you weren't looking forward to gardening in the summer."

"Nope."

Miles veered along the sidewalk that ran alongside the single-car garage that Ethan wasn't sure his truck would fit inside. "The cottage is back here. Nothing too fancy. It's small, but there's just you."

"Yep," Ethan said, his voice the cheery sort of hollow that made his heart twist. "Just me." The cottage came into view as Miles stepped under the roof that connected the back of the garage to another small structure.

Miles extracted a set of keys and unlocked the front door. He pushed it open and gestured for Ethan to go in first. Ethan glanced around, taking in little details—curtains on all the windows, already furnished with unfrilly items, a full-sized fridge and stove in the kitchen to his right—as his eyes adjusted to the darker quarters.

A sense of rightness filled his chest. He toured the single bedroom behind the living room. He liked how the bathroom attached to his room and the front room. The kitchen, while small, still provided him with everything he needed to put together a meal for one.

In truth, the cottage reminded him of his cabin in Three Rivers. A sharp twist of homesickness hit him, and again he wondered if Colorado Springs could make him happy.

"So I have two more—"

"I'll take this one," Ethan said.

"You sure?" Miles raised his eyebrows. "I scheduled the whole morning for you. There's two other places that are much more suited for apartment-style living."

The thought of having neighbors only a wall away suddenly made Ethan shiver. "No, this is great." He glanced around again, fondness overcoming him. "When can I move in?"

ETHAN SLID HIS FRIED EGGS OUT OF THE PAN AND ONTO ONE OF THE three plates he'd found in the cupboard. It had taken him an hour to get back to his mom's place and pack his pajamas. Then another few minutes to bring in the few boxes and bags he'd brought from Three Rivers. A bit longer to navigate to the nearest grocery store so he could make it through the weekend without eating out for every meal, and he was officially moved in.

Now, he sat in his new cottage, with steaming eggs and a couple of slices of toast that had just popped out of the toaster.

As he sat at the small table to eat, his thoughts wandered

down the block to Brynn's house. Ethan hadn't seen much on his walk the previous night, but enough to know they owned a lot of land and had filled it with barns and horses. Enough to know why Brynn was a cowgirl and a champion barrel racer. Enough to form a suspicion of why she couldn't quit, even if she wanted to. She'd never said she wanted to but had hinted at it.

He hadn't heard the rest of the conversation after she'd stomped up the stairs to the deck. He couldn't really see her through the branches of the surrounding trees, even though they bore no concealing leaves. He didn't want to know what else Brynn had said. What he'd heard had been damaging enough.

His phone sat inches from his left hand, and Ethan kept eyeing it like it might spring and bite at any moment. He finished eating and picked up his cell. He flipped it over and over, working up the courage to call Brynn.

Just to say hello, he told himself.

Yeah, right, the rational side of his brain said. *There's more to it than that.*

Maybe I'll tell her we're neighbors.

Do not ask her out.

I'm not going to ask her out.

But really, Ethan didn't know that for sure. A smile curved his lips as he found her name and pressed call.

She answered on the first ring. "Hello?"

His grin hitched. Didn't she have his number in her phone?

"Is this a prank call, Ethan? I assumed men of your age were past this." The teasing lilt in her voice set his nerves on fire.

"Oh, hey," he said, like the line had just connected.

"Oh, hey," she repeated. "You called me."

"Yeah, about that." He cleared his throat, trying to dislodge the traitorous words climbing toward his vocal chords. He'd already eaten—he was *not* going to ask her to dinner. "Wondering if you'd thought more about what I asked a few weeks ago."

"I've had a lot of conversations the past few weeks," she said.
"Remind me what we talked about."

"You know," Ethan said. "You helpin' me out with the rodeo stuff. Who's who, that kind of thing."

"Tanner—"

"I don't want Tanner to do it," Ethan said. "I just moved in down the street from you, and I want you—" His voice stumbled as the words fell from his mouth. "—to do it."

"You moved in down the street from me? How do you even know where I live?"

"I was with Tanner last night."

"And you didn't come in?"

"He said he had business with you. He didn't invite me to come with him."

"Where do you live?"

"'Bout half a block east, in Mrs. Berkley's cottage."

"Well," she said, her voice back to fun and flirty. "That's great, Ethan. Mrs. Berkley is a real nice lady."

"Seemed so," he said. He'd only met her for ten minutes to sign a contract and give her a bunch of money for rent and a deposit.

"So," Ethan pressed. "Will you do it? Training starts in a few days, and I'd like to know who to watch out for, who to trust, and what I can expect come Monday morning."

She remained silent so long, Ethan's hopes dashed to pieces on his new tiled floor. "Okay, well, that's fine," he said. "Maybe I will ask Tanner."

"I didn't say no."

"I haven't heard you say yes." Frustration built beneath Ethan's tongue. He needed to hang up before he said something to drive her further away.

Still, she wouldn't confirm to help him.

"How about this?" he asked. "You come over tomorrow morning, and I'll make us breakfast. Maybe then you'll be able to give me a firm yes or no on the topic."

Her silence unnerved him, made him want to throw down the phone and march over there to speak with her face-to-face.

"Nine o'clock," he said. "If you come, you come. We can talk."

"Okay," ghosted through the phone.

He chuckled. "It's not like I'll be makin' anything special, cowgirl. You allergic to eggs or something?"

"No," she snapped.

"Great," he said, glad she'd seemingly graduated from her catatonic state. "See you tomorrow." He hung up before she could confirm or deny that she'd be there.

Sleep took a while to claim him, mostly because he was in a new place, with new sounds, and new smells. Finally, he reminded himself that he wasn't living with his mother, and that allowed him to drift into unconsciousness with Brynn's beautiful face swirling in his mind.

5

B rynn checked her hair one more time, a slow anger burning through her body that someone like Ethan Greene had driven her to double-check her appearance. She normally braided her hair, stuck on her hat, and went out to get Washington saddled up for his warm-up ride.

Today, everything was off-schedule. And really, she did take a more leisurely approach to Saturdays, so a breakfast out with a friend wouldn't put her behind.

A friend. She watched herself as the words floated through her mind. Ethan could definitely become a friend. His quiet, yet thoughtful manner called to the chaos she felt in her life, an anchor of sorts she wished she could grab onto and never let go.

"Ridiculous," she scoffed at herself as she turned away from her reflection. She barely knew Ethan, and he was a cowboy. Still, she put on her boots and walked the half-block to Mrs. Berkley's before she knew she'd even moved.

He'd said he lived in the cottage behind the main house, and she stuck to the edges of the driveway, closest to where the tree branches had partially protected the ground from the snow. She moved around a stand-alone garage and found the place that must be Ethan's.

Her feet froze, but her blood ran hot. Something sweet wafted on the air, and her stomach growled, the traitor.

Brynn might as well admit that she wanted to see Ethan this morning, find out if he could cook a decent breakfast, tell him everything he needed to know about the other cowboys on the rodeo circuit. If she didn't, someone else would. Or he'd learn through a painful lesson—a painful lesson she could prevent.

She stepped up to the door and knocked, her fist loud in the winter silence. A few seconds went by. A few more. Brynn's unease grew, and she glanced over her shoulder for some sign that he was home.

The door whipped open, causing her to twist back to the house. Ethan stood there, and as time passed, he leaned against the doorframe and kicked a smile at her.

He wore jeans that stretched down his long legs and covered his cowboy boots. His short-sleeved polo wouldn't fly in Colorado Springs's brutal weather, but he seemed unfazed by the temperatures. His blond hair reminded her of a field of ripe wheat, and she appreciated that he hadn't yet covered his head with a cowboy hat.

"Mornin'," he finally said, stepping back. "You want to come in?"

"Yes." She shook herself and snapped her eyes away. "Yeah." She moved past him into the small space, which didn't seem cramped. "Wow, this is a nice place."

"Yeah." He stayed by the door as he closed it. "I got really lucky to get it."

"I didn't even know she rented." Brynn took in the neutral furniture and classy appliances. If she'd known, she might have snatched this place off the market. Not that she minded living with her father so much, but she certainly didn't have a home of her own. Nowhere she could go where she could brew her own specialty teas and spend time looking at new hairstyles.

"Coffee?" he asked as he slid by her and entered the kitchen. "Or tea?"

"Tea," she said, wondering how he knew the exact move to make.

He opened a cupboard and pulled out three boxes. "I have orange chamomile." He peered at the boxes, and Brynn knew he hadn't bought the tea. The way he studied the words made her chuckle at the same time a rush of adoration filled her mind.

"That one's darjeerling," she said. "And I love it. I'll take that."

He glanced away from the teas, a measure of relief shining in his eyes. "So you know how to make tea, then?"

Her chuckle turned into a full-on laugh. She stepped closer to him and took the tea from his fingers. "Yeah, I know how to make this."

"Good, because I've never had a drop of tea." He flashed her a grin that seemed nervous around the edges. "I already have hot water on." He indicated the steaming teapot on the stove.

"Teacup?" she asked.

He snapped into action, opening cupboards until he found the one with cups. "Doesn't look like I have any of those." He reached for something. "But I have mugs." He produced two, and she took the smaller of the two cups.

"You drink coffee?" she asked.

"Religiously," he said, pouring hot water into his mug and adding instant coffee granules.

Brynn winced. "That's how you make it?"

"How do you make it?" He kept his concentration on melting his instant coffee into his water.

"Not like that." She scooped a spoonful of tea leaves into her mug and covered them with a dose of hot water from the pot.

"So not even my coffee meets your standards." He glared at her for the space of a breath before turning around to collect a set

of oven mitts. He pulled a pan of cinnamon rolls out of the oven
—the source of the sweet smell she'd experienced outside.

Her stomach roared again, and Brynn stirred her tea to
distract herself. "I never said your coffee didn't meet my standards," she said. "I don't even like coffee."

"Of course you don't," he muttered.

Brynn didn't know what that meant, and her first instinct was
to demand to know the meaning of such words. But she pressed
her lips together and opened the cupboard to find a second mug.
She was tired of arguing with everyone she came in contact with.
She just wanted to enjoy her tea—and maybe her company. If
only Ethan was more suited to her. But it seemed they didn't have
a single thing in common—not even breakfast beverages.

"Do you like cinnamon rolls?" he asked, practically throwing
the oven mitts back on the counter.

"Of course," she said. "Bread, sugar, and butter. What's not
to like?"

His shoulders loosened; the edge in his eyes softened. "Okay,
then." He collected a couple of plates and placed them on the
table. After grabbing a bowl of fruit from the fridge, he used the
oven mitts to transfer the pan of rolls from the stovetop to the
tabletop.

He sat down and looked at her. "You need two mugs to
make tea?"

Brynn startled as she finished dumping out the hot water
she'd poured into the second mug to warm it. "Sort of."

He chuckled and shook his head while she poured the
steeped tea from the first cup into the second, using the back of
her spoon to keep the spent leaves in the first cup. She joined him
at the table-built-for-two, trying not to panic about how close
they were. But she could feel the heat from his body, smell the
crispness of his aftershave, see the flecks of teal in his blue eyes.

He served her an ooey, gooey cinnamon roll and nudged a
fork closer to her. "So tell me about the bull riders you know."

She sucked in a breath and stuck a huge bite of pastry into her mouth to buy herself some time to find an answer. She knew he wanted an insider's perspective on the rodeo, but she hadn't prepared anything for him.

He watched her for eons past comfortable, and she finally managed to swallow. "Do you always stare at your guests?"

"When they're as pretty as you," he said, leaning forward.

A flush started in her chest and rose. He jerked away as if she'd thrown her piping hot tea in his face and leapt to his feet.

"Sorry," he muttered.

"It's fine," she said, a teasing lilt in her voice. If he wanted to call her pretty, she wasn't going to stop him. She craved attention —no, not just attention. *His* attention.

The realization made her reach for her tea and gulp a scalding mouthful. "So you know Tanner," she started. "He's the loudest rider on the circuit, and he can usually back up what he says."

Ethan leaned against the counter in the corner of the kitchen as far from Brynn as he could get. She wondered what she'd done wrong, why he'd leapt away from her after calling her pretty, how to break through the ice that now frosted his expression. She didn't know, so she talked and talked and talked.

EVERY MUSCLE IN ETHAN'S BODY SCREAMED FOR A RELEASE. HE'D been holding them so tight, so tight, as he listened to Brynn detail the various riders and ropers he'd meet next week. She sipped that soft pink tea, drawing his attention to her mouth over and over again.

He was going to go mad, absolutely crazy, before she finished. He closed his eyes and focused on the smooth, sexy quality of her voice.

"...Milt Jackson is the defending bronc rider. And he's a bit of a...he's a little arrogant. I'd stay out of his way if I were you."

"You know all these guys?" he asked, opening his eyes to find her watching him. He gripped the edge of the countertop until his knuckles ached.

"Yeah, I know 'em," she said. "Been out with a few of them. Now I try to avoid almost everyone."

Ethan sensed a deep history between Brynn and everyone he'd meet on Monday. But he didn't want to ask about who she'd dated previously. He just wanted to know if she was seeing anyone now.

"Everyone?" he asked. "You're obviously friends with Tanner."

"Tanner is different."

Of course he was. Ethan wanted to know in what way, but he kept his mouth shut. Brynn was talking, and he liked the sound of it better than he would his questions about the status of their relationship. Still, why she had some of Tanner's keys, and why she'd driven almost six hours to come talk Ethan into joining the PRCA, needled his mind, puncturing it until her words warbled and warped in his mind.

"Oh, wow," she finally said. "It's almost lunchtime." She stood, the scratch of her chair against tile making Ethan cringe. "I need to go."

"Yeah, sure," he said. "What are your afternoon plans?"

She shrugged into her coat. "Training with my horse." She tossed her dark braid over her shoulder and zipped her jacket. Her movement stalled and she met his gaze. The world seemed to narrow until it contained only him and her, and Ethan couldn't look away even if he wanted to.

But he didn't want to.

"It's Saturday night," she started before her voice went silent. She swallowed and the healthy blush stained her cheeks, driving Ethan near his breaking point.

"You could come see my horse this afternoon and stay for

dinner." She rushed through the invitation, but Ethan caught all the words.

"Daddy makes ribs on Saturday nights, and they're pretty good. I mean, if you like ribs. He makes his own barbeque sauce and everything. Probably started it an hour ago." She took a breath, but it wasn't enough time for Ethan to say anything. "You don't have to. I mean, you've seen horses before. And probably eaten a million ribs." She turned toward the front door. "Of course you have. You work on a cattle ranch, and—" She cut off as he placed one hand on the door just above her shoulder.

She lifted her eyes to meet his, and he could lean down and touch his lips to hers if he were still the old Ethan. The one who would've asked her out that first night in Texas. The one who would've come to Colorado Springs just because she was the one asking.

But he was a new man now, and he didn't want to be the person he'd been before. "I'd like to meet your horse," he said, real slow so he wouldn't give her the wrong idea about anything. "What's his name?"

"Washington," she breathed, swaying toward him slightly. Heat burned between them, and Ethan felt confident if he asked her out right now, she'd say yes.

Don't do it, he coached himself.

"Washington? After the president?" he asked instead.

"One of my high school teachers." One corner of her mouth curled up, making Ethan's palms sweat. "She taught home economics, and she did nails on the side. I loved going to her salon and getting a pedicure." She smiled fully, her mind some-where in the past. "Miss Washington. She moved just before I left traditional school to join the professional circuit."

Questions burned through Ethan. He hadn't pegged Brynn for a girly-type woman who liked getting her hair and nails done, but at the same time, such things fit her.

He nodded and added his grin to the conversation. "We have

a horse named Houdini back on the ranch. That thing." He laughed, the sound true and striking a chord in his heart. "He could get out of anything. He really was a magician."

Brynn laughed with him. "Sounds like a troublemaker."

"Oh, he is," Ethan said. "But he was still a real good horse."

The mood sobered, and Ethan put some space between himself and Brynn. "Thanks for comin'. And I haven't had ribs in a long time. What time should I come over?"

She took a deep, deep breath. "I'll be in the arena until five-thirty. Daddy serves dinner at six-thirty. I shower in that hour, so if you don't want to submit yourself to my brothers and my father, come at six-thirty. Otherwise, anytime this afternoon is fine." She ducked her head, her fingers fumbling for the doorknob.

"This afternoon, then," he said, a thread of trepidation pulling through him at the thought of meeting her family. Of joining the professional rodeo circuit in just two days. Of starting something with Brynn he might not be around to finish.

6

Brynn tired of training by four o'clock, but she'd told Ethan she'd be out in the horse arena until five-thirty. She'd been watching for him since the moment she arrived in the barn—ridiculous, but she didn't even try to keep the truth from invading her mind.

It had been a long time since Brynn had been out with a man, and eating breakfast and talking about the rodeo that morning had brought a balm to her soul she desperately needed. Though she and Ethan seemed made from opposite ends of the universe, she couldn't help feeling drawn to him. The same way a north pole attracted a south.

She sighed and dismounted. Washington could tell her thoughts lingered somewhere else, and he tossed his head in displeasure. It took two to ride and win the barrel race, and Brynn patted him. "I know, boy. Sorry."

Pressing her forehead to his, she exhaled out her anxiety over Ethan's late arrival. Her frustration at having to put in the hours so her father wouldn't ask questions. Her resentment at starting another rodeo season instead of actually living the life she wanted.

"One more year," she whispered to herself and the horse. "I'm only doing this for one more year."

"Am I interrupting?"

She spun at the deep voice behind her. Ethan wore his charcoal gray cowboy hat, which hid his strong features in shadows.

Brynn managed a weak chuckle. "No, c'mon over."

He passed through a shrinking patch of sunlight coming in from the skylights in the roof. His boots brought him closer and closer, and her mind went more and more numb.

"Looked like you were tellin' this horse some secrets." He took the reins from her, and she let him.

"Maybe I was." She infused her voice with singsong.

"Want to tell me?" He slid her a flirtatious glance. She hadn't imagined the current between them at his place, because it sparked just as strongly now.

"Maybe later," she said, but she didn't plan to tell anyone what she'd confessed to Washington. No one could know she intended to walk away until after the very last event. She couldn't risk even a rumor of her quitting the rodeo to circulate—or get back to her father.

Ethan began to walk Washington around the arena, and Brynn went with them. The sound of the horse's hooves and Ethan's steady breathing created a peaceful atmosphere Brynn hadn't felt in the arena for a while.

"How's your mom?" she asked to break the silence between them.

"Doin' just fine."

"You didn't stay with her long."

A frown flitted across Ethan's face. "No, I didn't."

"Why not?"

He cast a long look in her direction. "You always so nosy?" He grinned, which took most of the sting from his words.

"Not usually," she said. "Maybe I just want to—" She sucked

in the remainder of her sentence when his hand brushed hers. On his next step, he captured her fingers in his.

"I don't mind," he said.

They stepped, stepped, stepped, her hand still resting comfortably in his.

"So you didn't stay with your mom for very long..." she prompted.

He dropped her hand, and every cell in Brynn's fingers turned cold.

"I'm too old to live with my mother," he said.

"That's not the real reason," Brynn said, unsure of where the words came from. They just felt true. Oh, and the way he wouldn't meet her eye spoke volumes, as had the false quality of his voice.

He gave a short laugh. "You're right, it's not. My mother is...a special breed. I can only handle her in small doses."

"I get that," she said.

"Do you?" He peered at her, but she kept her attention on her boots. "You live with your whole family, don't you?"

She nodded. "It's okay. I manage to get away from them when I need to."

"By hiding out in the arena and whispering to horses."

She smiled against her will, the way he spoke with such a lightness to his tone conveying that he wasn't making fun of her or judging her.

"A girl's gotta do what a girl's gotta do."

"You could get your own apartment," he said. "Washington won't even know the difference."

"Daddy will," she said before she could censor herself.

"Ah, so you don't like living with him any more than I liked living with my mother."

"I didn't say that."

"You didn't need to."

Brynn stayed quiet as she thought about moving out of her

bedroom. Her childhood home had been in Dallas, but she'd never moved away from her dad or her brothers. They'd moved here just over ten years ago, and while Chuck and Duke dated from time to time, they weren't serious about getting married and leaving their lives behind. Chuck retired from the rodeo last year, but traveled with Brynn and planned to take over her career when Daddy got too old. Duke boarded horses right here on the property. His very successful, busy boarding house kept him attending to animals all day long.

Brynn couldn't seem to think about anything but leaving this life behind. Well, maybe not the marrying bit, but definitely leaving the rodeo behind.

"Can I ask you something?" Ethan led Washington toward the back of the arena, where the horse stalls waited. How he knew, Brynn wasn't sure.

Maybe he's a horseman and not a cowboy, she thought.

They're the same thing, she chastised herself. She couldn't let herself off the no-cowboy hook on a technicality.

"Sure," she said.

"Where's the closest church?" He cleared his throat. "I want to go tomorrow. Try to calm down before I have to start the rodeo thing on Monday."

Surprise flitted through Brynn's system. "Church, huh?" She scanned him, more to take in the magnificent sight of him than to find something she couldn't see. "I didn't think someone like you would be into church."

"Someone like me?" He paused and raised his eyebrows.

She took Washington's reins, almost brushing her fingers across Ethan's as she did. Her teeth ground together with the effort it took not to touch him. She hated the feeling of being out of control, of being pulled toward this man she didn't want to be attracted to.

"You know," she said, squirming under the weight of his continued gaze.

"No, I don't know."

"I just don't know a lot of cowboys that go to church." She unlatched the gate that led to the stalls and moved in front of Washington, effectively putting too much distance between her and Ethan to continue the conversation.

He followed her, though, arriving in the small space only a few minutes after she'd started to unsaddle her horse.

"I know a lot of cowboys that go to church," he said. "Lots of 'em at Three Rivers attend every week."

She shrugged, unable to vocalize anything more that wouldn't make her seem even more rude.

"So you don't know a church nearby." He wasn't asking, and when she looked at him, he had those muscular arms crossed, making his biceps bulge.

Brynn did—the one she attended from time to time. Her face heated for the tenth time that day—but this time not because of something Ethan said or one of his swoon-worthy smiles. But because she hadn't actually darkened the doorway of her church for a few months now. How ridiculous would she look showing up tomorrow, just because Ethan was going?

"It's okay," he said. "My mom's not super religious, but maybe—"

"Neither's my daddy," she said. "I go a little bit, but I haven't been in a while." She pulled the brush across Washington's back. "Mostly because I don't want to have to explain myself to him."

Several strokes later, and she finished with the horse. The silence in the small room suffocated her, stole all the oxygen, until she wanted to scream just to infuse some sound into the air.

"Brynn," Ethan said in that soft, strong voice of his. "You're an adult. You can do whatever you want."

Tears pricked her eyes. He had no idea how wrong he was. Her life wasn't hers to live. It hadn't been since the day her momma had died. After that, everything and everyone aimed at pleasing Daddy. Even Duke and Chuck had given up things they wanted to keep Daddy happy.

"Brynn." Ethan moved closer. His fingers trailed up her jacketed arm and nudged her chin up until her watery eyes looked into his fierce ones. "Do you want to come to church with me tomorrow?"

Her heart leapt at the prospect, stalled at the thought of sitting so close to him for so long, yearned to get back inside the walls of a building where she felt loved and appreciated. Or at least she had when Momma took her.

She hadn't felt loved or appreciated in a long time. At least not just for being herself. For being a champion barrel racer, sure. But not just because she was Brynn Bowman. Oh, no. Just being Brynn was never enough—for anyone.

Ethan's fingers followed her tears down her face, wiping them away and igniting a fire deep in her core at the same time. "You pick me up, and drive us there, and we'll sit by each other. Deal?"

She nodded, sucking back the emotion she'd allowed to show.

"Brynn?"

At the sound of Chuck's voice, she jumped and immediately put as much distance between her and Ethan as possible.

"Yeah," she said, her voice still somewhat painted with tears.

"Just lookin' for you," he said. "You're always in the same place at the same time."

Good ol' reliable Brynn, she thought with a measure of bitterness that hadn't felt so palpable before.

"A friend of mine came to meet Washington." She swiped at her eyes and stepped around Ethan. "Ethan, this is my oldest brother, Chuck. Chuck, this is Ethan. He's joining the rodeo circuit as Tanner's header."

Chuck appraised Ethan the way all big brothers did. One cocked eyebrow. Dubious edge riding in his eye. But something else flared there too. Brynn couldn't decide if it was hope or pity before Chuck moved forward and shook Ethan's hand.

"Nice to meet you." He tilted his head to the side, his eyes narrowing. "You look familiar. We met before?"

ETHAN'S STOMACH SETTLED SOMEWHERE NEAR THE SOLES OF HIS feet. What had he done to be cursed that the very first person he met would know him from his previous rodeo days? And not just someone—Brynn's brother.

"Brynn says you rode in the rodeo?" Ethan asked.

Chuck exchanged a glance with Brynn. "Started bronc ridin' 'bout nine years ago, I think. Retired last year."

"Last time I rode was six years ago. So we'd have overlapped a bit." Ethan wanted to leave the arena, right now, but he didn't allow his feet to so much as shuffle. He'd have to endure meeting people who'd been on the circuit the last time he was, plain and simple.

Chuck snapped his fingers. "Bull rider. Champion, if I remember right."

"Not that last year." Ethan made his voice as even as possible.

"No...the year before. And the year before that." Chuck smiled, Ethan's championships obviously a check mark in the pro column. He certainly hadn't felt that way while the other cowboy sized him up and wondered what Ethan was doing with his sister.

"Is that true?" Brynn stepped to Chuck's side, her eyes wide and innocent.

"Yes," Ethan clipped out.

"No wonder Tanner wanted you," Brynn said.

Did she want him now too? Because of the championships he'd won eight years ago? An invisible blade sliced through Ethan's chest.

I hope not, he thought.

Don't get your hopes up, the rational side of his brain warned. *Everyone loves a champion, especially one who can conquer bulls.*

Not Brynn, he argued with himself. *She's different.*

Is she? Look how she's staring at you, all goo-goo eyed and adoring.

Ethan looked, and he didn't like what he saw. He'd fantasized since she'd left at noon about the way she might one day look at him with that level of adoration in her expression. But he most certainly didn't want it because he been a champion bull rider eight long years ago.

"It's been a long time since I rode a bull," he said. "Now, I believe you said something about ribs."

"You invited him to dinner?" The level of incredulity in Chuck's voice didn't fall on deaf ears.

Brynn slapped him on the bicep. "Of course I did. He just moved here and doesn't have anything to eat." She tossed a look that said, *I'm sorry. I know you can take care of yourself,* in his direction, and he ducked his head as he smiled.

"But Daddy—"

"Loves guests," Brynn said over Chuck. "Come on. You can entertain Ethan while I shower."

ETHAN'S PLANS OF HOLDING BRYNN'S HAND UNTIL THEY CAME INTO view of her house got dashed to pieces as she strode next to her brother, leaving Ethan to follow in their wake. At least Ethan now knew the man was Brynn's brother and not some boyfriend he'd have to compete with. It occurred to him that he still didn't know if Brynn was seeing anyone or not.

Of course she's not, he thought. *She let you hold her hand in the arena.*

But he knew that didn't mean much. She'd been vulnerable. Caught whispering something she didn't want anyone to overhear. Still, he hadn't invented the chemistry between them. She felt something just like he did. If she had a boyfriend, well, Ethan wouldn't know what he'd do. He knew what the old Ethan would do, but this was new territory for his reformed self.

Brynn entered the house and scampered down a hall, leaving Ethan in a bright, cheery kitchen that reminded him of the homestead at Three Rivers Ranch. A tall, wide-shouldered man stood at the stove, stirring something.

"Dad," Chuck said. "This is a friend of Brynn's. He's stayin' for dinner."

The man turned, and Ethan saw where Brynn got her nose. Beyond that, she must've had the more delicate features of her mother, because this man had deep blue eyes set below a weathered, lined forehead.

"Welcome," he said, flashing a quick smile. "I'm Walt Bowman."

"Ethan Greene." He stepped forward and shook the man's hand. "Brynn says you make your own barbeque sauce."

Walt's chest swelled. "Putting the finishing touches on now. We're doin' ribs in the oven because the grill's buried under two feet of snow."

"We could always move back to Texas," Chuck said, a glint in his eye.

Walt grumbled something about never going back, and Chuck gave Ethan a mock shrug. Ethan grinned, quickly wiping the emotion away when Walt turned and asked him how he knew Brynn.

"Through the rodeo," Ethan said.

Walt frowned as he bent to open the oven. "Thought I knew all the boys on the circuit."

"He's new, Dad," Chuck said. "Startin' this year. Gonna be Tanner's header."

A rush of gratitude that Chuck hadn't mentioned his previous rodeo career flowed through Ethan.

"He's still doin' that ropin' business?" Walt set the enormous platter of ribs on the stovetop and began basting them with the barbeque sauce.

"He won last year, Dad."

Walt harrumphed, and Ethan catalogued his opinion of roping for reference later. Chuck set the table while Walt sliced winter squash and started sautéing it.

Ethan didn't quite know what to do, or what to say, so he lingered by the door. Another man—clearly another of Brynn's brothers, with the same dark hair and boxy chin as his father—entered the room.

"You won't believe what Teddy—" He cut off when he spied Ethan. "Oh, hey."

"This is Ethan," Chuck said. "Brynn's friend."

"Brynn's *friend*?" This man clearly didn't trust anyone who called themselves a friend of Brynn's. Ethan wondered what would happen if he said he was thinking about being more than friends with Brynn.

"She's twenty-five. She's allowed to have friends." Chuck rolled his eyes. "This is Duke. The more protective, yet younger, brother."

"There's just the two of you?" Ethan asked.

Duke scowled, and Chuck laughed. "And Dad," he said.

"How are you and Brynn friends?" Duke asked.

"Rodeo," Chuck and Ethan said together.

That answer made Duke visibly relax, and Ethan remembered Chuck had done the same in the arena. Why didn't they think Ethan could graduate beyond friendship with Brynn simply because they'd met through the rodeo?

I'm just not into cowboys.

Her earlier words slammed into his mind as he recalled them. So she'd had bad experiences dating men in the rodeo circuit. Had probably told her family she was done with all cowboys because of it.

Fair enough.

He'd let them think what they wanted for now. But all their reactions did was fuel the fire that flickered inside him. The fire that wanted to be with Brynn, show her that some cowboys were worth spending time with.

Help me be that man, he prayed as she reappeared in the kitchen, her hair still damp and her cheeks still flushed from the heat of the shower.

She cast him a worried look, her gaze flying from man to man in the kitchen. She finally settled on Ethan, the question evident in her eyes. *Everything okay?*

He gave her his most charming smile as her dad announced, "Dinner's ready."

7

Brynn's nerves hadn't settled since Ethan showed up in the arena yesterday afternoon. Sure, she'd felt that momentary peace when he held her hand and wiped her tears. She got flustered just thinking about how she'd shown him her vulnerabilities—and what he might do with them.

She hadn't had much luck with the men she'd dated. They'd been rough-and-tumble cowboys, and any sign of weakness usually sent them running for the hills. But Ethan hadn't done that. He'd been conversational and kind during dinner. He'd laughed at her father's corny jokes and asked Duke about the new horse until Brynn wanted to scream.

He'd seemed truly interested in her family, in her.

And that had kept her skin buzzing and her nerves humming all night long.

"And now you have to go to church with him," she muttered to herself as she tried to find something appropriate for church in her closet. She owned more jeans and boots than skirts and heels, but she managed to find a navy bow skirt that looked decent enough with a black and white striped blouse. She slipped her feet into a dark pair of heels and wobbled down the hall to the kitchen, ready for Daddy's brows to droop and his mouth to set into a tight line.

He hadn't been a fan of religion since Momma died, but he'd allowed Brynn to attend whenever she felt like it. And like Ethan had reminded her, she was an adult, and she could do what she wanted.

So she stretched up to kiss Daddy's cheek like she always did. He glanced down at her like he always did. "Church today, huh?" he asked, that V appearing between his eyes.

"Yeah. I told Ethan I'd show him where it was."

Daddy grunted and refocused on the scrambled eggs. Brynn cursed herself for mentioning Ethan. Daddy wouldn't be the one to fire questions at her, but by the time she returned from church, Duke and Chuck would have their attack all planned out.

She grabbed a protein bar from the pantry. "I'm gonna be late, so I'll just eat this on the way." In truth, she didn't think her rumbling stomach could hold anything down. "I'll be back in time for a late lunch and then I'll spend the afternoon with Washington."

"All right." He didn't turn or look at her as she clicked toward the exit. Once in the safety of her four-wheel-drive, she exhaled, the first release of nervousness she'd allowed herself since waking.

Ethan stood on the curb when she pulled up. "Hey," he said as he opened the passenger door. "I saw you leave."

"You did?" She craned her neck to even see the corner of the cottage that sat down the lane and behind the garage.

"Maybe I was just antsy waiting inside." His face held the pinkness of a man who'd been outside for a while, and the way he fisted his hands and kept them in his pockets testified of the same thing.

"I told you I'd be here at nine-thirty," she said, cranking the heat.

"Yeah." He looked at her. "I just went for a walk. Don't like walls much."

She nodded and put the car in drive. "Okay, so I have a confession."

He chuckled, and the bass sound of it sent vibrations through her heartbeat. "Finally. The juicy stuff."

"Don't get excited," she teased. "I just haven't been to church in a while." Her words hung in the air for a few breaths.

"You could've just given me the address," he said. "I have a car."

"Oh, I don't mind goin'," she said quickly. "I just wanted to warn you that, well, the pastor might act surprised to see me."

"He'll probably be happy to see you." Ethan unpocketed one of his hands and reached for hers. He masterfully slid his fingers in between hers. "I know I am."

Heat shot to the top of her head, and Brynn felt sure the temperature in the car had risen fifty degrees. She squeezed his hand. "Thanks."

He grinned and settled their joined hands on the console between them. He suddenly pulled his hand away. "Okay, I have a confession too."

She glanced at him and then back to the road. "Yeah?"

"I've been dyin' to know if you're dating anyone." He gestured between them. "I don't really want to get used to holdin' your hand only to find out you've got a cowboy boyfriend on the rodeo circuit."

Brynn burst out laughing, unable to contain the absurdity of his statement. "I don't date cowboys," she said, realizing a heartbeat too late what she'd said.

His hands went right back in his pockets, and he focused his attention out the windshield. "Okay, then."

"I mean—" But she didn't know what she meant. She certainly had a no-cowboy policy, especially since Dave. She'd just told Chuck this very thing a few nights ago. How had Ethan undone her conviction in only a couple short days?

She pulled into the church parking lot, her mind churning and her gut roiling and her mouth about to spill all the words she'd been trying to arrange into an explanation. She cut the engine, and Ethan reached for the door handle.

Employing a tactic he'd done the first time they rode in a car together, Brynn slapped the automatic locks into place, causing Ethan to swing his gaze toward her. She lost herself in the depth of his stormy eyes for just a moment. "Okay, look," she said. "I used to date cowboys, and they're mostly jerks."

He flinched at her words and started nodding. "I get it, Brynn. No explanation needed."

"Yes, I do need to explain." Her fingers worried themselves over each other, the ghost of his touch still skating along her skin. "But you don't seem like the other cowboys I've dated, and I like spending time with you."

Feeling daring and brave and everything Brynn only was while barrel racing, she reached for his hand. He let her take it, intertwine her fingers through his. A sigh passed through her body at his calming touch. "I don't have a cowboy boyfriend on the rodeo circuit." She lifted her eyes to his, dropped all her pretenses. "Yet."

A delicious smile curved his mouth. He squeezed her hand, and then lifted it to his lips. A riot of crows flapped in her chest and everything in her wanted to touch her lips to his.

"Okay, then," he said. "Let's go see what your pastor has to say."

Brynn woke to the sound of an alarm, and Ethan continued to dominate her thoughts for a few minutes as she journeyed toward consciousness. As the pleasant dreams of him holding her hand ebbed into the recesses of her mind, she remembered that today was Monday, that she was due at the riders' meeting later that morning.

And Ethan would be there.

She contained her smile as she showered, but her brain and body still knew they'd be seeing Ethan in a very short while. She took extra care with her hair and makeup, something she tried to tell herself she would've done anyway. It was the first day of the new season, after all.

By the time she showed up at the hotel where the PRCA had rented a couple of conference rooms, her heart bobbed in the back of her throat. Ethan had told her the previous afternoon that he would be going with Tanner, and Brynn hoped they'd be here already. She hated walking into a room by herself, without the thought that she'd be able to find someone she knew and could make herself part of a group.

She reminded herself that she had girlfriends on the circuit—the other girls she raced against. They were all cordial, even if they wanted to beat her at every event.

The group met together in the ballroom for the first half of the day, and then they'd be split into their events, where they'd get more specific instructions. Brynn waited in line to check in, trying not to be too obvious about searching for someone she knew.

Not just someone. Ethan.

She didn't find him before she stepped up to the table and gave the volunteer her name. She received her name badge, which listed her registered events, and a folder full of papers, and a bottle of water. She took everything with her into the ballroom, the enormity of the room reminding her of the vastness of the rodeo arenas she raced in. She always felt small and insignificant in the few seconds before she spurred Washington into his fastest gallop and tightest turns.

Pastor Paul's words came back to her as she stood just inside the doorway, searching for a table where she could sit. *God wants to help you.*

She'd believed him when he'd spoken yesterday. He'd said it with such passion Brynn had felt it all the way down to her toes. But she'd puzzled through the sermon for the rest of the day. She didn't know what God wanted to help her to do. She was good at barrel racing. She made decent money. She loved horses and being outside.

But the idea of going to beauty school also pulled at her, called her in a different direction. One completely the opposite of the rodeo, and dirty boots, and only wearing jeans.

She pushed the thoughts away as she finally found Kami Yeager and stepped toward her table. The blonde cowgirl sat with another woman Brynn had never met, and they didn't seem to be talking much.

Brynn slid into the seat next to Kami, barely glancing at the other blonde. "Hey, Kami."

"Brynn!" Kami stood and Brynn did too so they could embrace. "It's so good to see you." She carried a heap of relief in her voice that Brynn didn't understand. They'd been friends, but not overly close. Brynn wasn't overly close with anyone except her brothers. Everything was easier that way.

They sat and Brynn opened her folder. She hadn't even been able to focus on the top paper—a calendar of sanctioned PRCA events across the country—when Kami said, "You remember Alyssa Shumway, don't you?"

The name opened a hole in Brynn's soul. She willed herself not to gasp, not to look up, but she did both anyway. She focused on the second blonde at the table, and as the heart-shaped face and striking green eyes sank into her vision, Brynn did indeed remember Alyssa Shumway.

"You're blonde now," was what she managed to say. "I didn't even recognize you."

The once redhead tossed her bleached curls over her shoulder. Both Kami and Brynn had opted for smarter, more sensible ponytails.

Leave it to Alyssa to be looking for a man more than a win, Brynn thought, her internal voice poisonous. No wonder Kami had sounded so relieved. If Brynn had been sitting at a table with Alyssa alone, she'd have done almost anything to escape.

"Are you doing the PRCA circuit this year?" Brynn asked. "Or just the women's rodeo?" In the past, Alyssa had opted to compete in only the Women's Professional Rodeo Association's women-only events. She'd done calf roping, bareback riding, and barrel racing, excelling at everything she entered.

A tang of jealousy coated Brynn's tongue as Alyssa said, "I'm just doing the barrel racing this year. National PRCA events."

So every event Brynn would be in. Her heart thumped against her breastbone. Maybe she should've been practicing harder these past few months. Or maybe she didn't care, as she'd be retiring at the end of this season no matter if she won or not.

The emcee for the session welcomed everyone to the general session, and Brynn turned away from her biggest competition. But Alyssa's eyes felt branded on the side of Brynn's face. They both knew why Alyssa had left three years ago—and only the two of them knew of Alyssa's inappropriate attachment to Brynn's once-fiancé.

The memories Brynn had worked so hard to forget paraded through her mind while she should've been focusing on what the president of the PRCA outlined. But all she could think about was Dave breaking things off with her so he could follow Alyssa wherever she happened to want to go.

———

ETHAN SUFFERED THROUGH THE LONGEST MEETING OF HIS LIFE, constantly searching the huge ballroom for any sign of Brynn. Not only couldn't he find her, he couldn't seem to shake Tanner for more than four seconds to really look. The man had somehow attached himself to Ethan, and he wasn't letting him out of his sight.

"After lunch, there will be individual meetings for specific events," the man at the podium said. "You can find room numbers in your folders, but there is one change...."

Ethan tuned him out. Tanner would get him where he needed to go for team roping and bull riding. He'd seen a couple of cowboys who were still in the profession from when he'd left. But he and Tanner had arrived so late, he hadn't been cornered by them yet. In the two breaks they'd had that morning, Tanner had kept him occupied. Ethan was grateful for that, even if it had frustrated his plans to find Brynn and talk to her.

He joined the line of cowboys collecting a boxed lunch, a vein of frustration flowing through him that everyone seemed so tall. He couldn't see around them to see if Brynn was nearby.

"Who you lookin' for?" Tanner asked from behind him.

Ethan's mind raced. "No one. Should I be lookin' for someone?"

"I already warned the older cowboys to leave you alone." His gaze bored into the side of Ethan's face, as if he somehow sensed Ethan hadn't told the truth.

"It's fine," Ethan said, inching closer to the table. "I can handle myself. Brynn already told me who was still here."

"Oh?" The interest in Tanner's voice grated across Ethan's already vibrating nerves. "When did you talk with the lovely Brynn Bowman?"

Ethan mentally berated himself for bringing her up. "You know. Here and there." No way he was telling Tanner anything about his afternoon in the arena with her, or eating dinner with her family, or going to church with her.

"You like her?" Tanner asked as Ethan reached for a water bottle.

He clenched it too tight to be casual. "Sure, I guess. Don't really know her."

"But you want to know her."

Ethan shrugged. "Not really that interested." He blindly took a box without checking to see what kind of sandwich it held. The sooner he could get away from Tanner, from this conversation, the better.

"Right," Tanner said. "You're always interested."

Ethan exhaled, wishing it as easy to show Tanner that he'd changed. That he wasn't the same guy he'd once been. "Not really, Tanner. I'm not the same guy I was last time you knew me."

Tanner shouldered him. "I know you better than you think."

"You really don't." Ethan snatched a napkin and a fork and turned on his heel to escape. He nearly smashed his box lunch into Henry Hansen's chest. "Sorry," he mumbled, desperate to disappear now.

"Ethan Greene," the cowboy boomed, causing everyone in the vicinity to turn in their direction. "I'd heard you were comin' back. Not sure I believed it."

Ethan raised his chin, a measure of his old pride returning at Henry's disdainful tone. "Helpin' out a friend for a year. That's all."

Henry's eyes swept past Ethan to find Tanner a half-step behind him. "You're Wolf's new header?"

"Yep," Tanner said, the word like a punch to the face.

Henry focused on Ethan again. "Bull riding too?"

"Yes."

Henry smiled, but it wasn't the friendly type. More like predatory. "Well, we'll be seein' a lot of each other then. Those are the two events I compete in."

"Fantastic," Ethan deadpanned. "Good to see you again." He stepped around the man and re-entered the ballroom, still looking for Brynn though he wished he could *stop already.*

AFTER A COUPLE MORE MEETINGS, TANNER FINALLY TOOK ETHAN away from the boring business side of rodeo and to the barn. "Horses here. You should pick yours and start training tonight. We'll start practicing in the morning."

Trepidation tripped through Ethan's bloodstream. He hadn't actually thrown a rope in a very long time. He'd been watching videos, and practicing the hand movements in his cottage. But none of that was actually the same as riding a bouncing horse and throwing a real rope at a moving target.

He wandered down the stalls, checking the horses for qualities and characteristics he liked, that he needed in a header horse. He'd need a tall, strong horse so he could veer left and pull the five-hundred-pound steer with him. But also one that was explosive and quick.

He ended up choosing a tall, broad, chestnut horse with white markings on his legs. "What's your name, huh?" he asked the horse as he stroked his mane.

"That's Tiger," Tanner said. "He's a good horse. Perfect for dallying and turning steer."

"I like 'im," Ethan said, feeling a bond with Tiger already. "I can use him?"

"Yeah, he belongs to the Saddlers. I'll talk to Ginny."

Ethan nodded, the Saddlers a common name among championship horses. They raised them, bred them to win, rented them to cowboys to earn more championships. "Where's his saddle?"

"Tack room through there. Ropes on the wall too."

"Thanks. You stayin' a while?"

"Yeah," Tanner said. "I'll come find you when I'm ready to go."

Ethan nodded and headed for the tack room. He saddled Tiger and tested the weight of the rope in his hand. He took Tiger out to the practice facility, but looped his reins around a fence before dragging a nearby calf dummy closer and tossing the rope in its direction.

To his surprise, his throw wasn't half-bad. Still, relief sank through him at the fact that he was alone. He didn't need eyewitnesses to his failures.

After a while, he managed to get the rope exactly where it needed to go. "Now to do it while riding." He swung into the saddle and Tiger responded to his gentle commands with ease. He rode the horse around the arena, just getting a feel for him, letting him get comfortable with Ethan.

He dismounted and put the calf dummy in the center of the arena, and positioned Tiger where he imagined the chute would be in a real rodeo event. He took a deep breath, pushing the pressure and anxiety from his mind, the way he'd have to during a real rodeo event.

He remembered the screaming fans, the bright lights, the loud music. He'd have to focus more than he had in years to perform the way he used to.

"Yup!" He urged Tiger into a sprint, his gaze singularly on the calf in the middle of the arena. He threw the rope...and missed.

He went through the ritual several more times, until he finally managed to loop the rope around the calf's horns.

Victorious, he brushed down Tiger and put the horse back in his stall. He didn't know where Tanner had disappeared to, but he wandered through the practice facilities and found cowboys practicing their bareback riding, their roping, their steer wrestling.

He didn't seen any women doing barrel racing, and he speculated that they might have a separate facility. The exit lay down one hall and around a corner. Up ahead, Ethan heard voices, and he hesitated. He didn't really want to encounter anyone here, not yet.

Fiddling with his phone, Ethan listened to the voices, finding one of them familiar. Definitely Tanner.

He continued toward the corner, lightening his steps for some reason he couldn't name. He rounded the corner and found Tanner and Brynn facing off several paces down the hallway. Ethan couldn't tell if either was angry, as they'd stopped speaking.

Tanner reached out and tucked an errant lock of Brynn's hair behind her ear. The tender gesture caused lightning to strike inside Ethan's chest. His insides turned cold and hollow as Tanner leaned down and touched his lips to Brynn's cheek before stepping past her and leaving the building.

Ethan stared at Brynn, first as she watched Tanner go, then as she lifted her hand to her cheek. She cradled it almost reverently, like he'd given her a treasured gift.

Sickness rose through Ethan, and he couldn't swallow away the bitterness coating his throat, his tongue.

Tanner had just kissed Brynn.

He spun away from her, from the exit where Tanner had gone, and strode back the way he'd come. He took several turns without thought, finding another door that led outside, where another building squatted in the winter darkness.

He pushed through the door and found himself in the stands above the barrel racing arena. He sat down, his mind frothing and his heart pounding and his stomach churning.

Time passed, but Ethan didn't know how much. Anger poisoned him, first at himself for being so stupid, and falling so fast, and thinking that sitting by Brynn at church and holding her hand a few times made them a couple.

Then at her for saying she didn't have a boyfriend on the rodeo circuit. He hadn't hallucinated that conversation in her SUV. Hadn't made up the squeeze she gave his hand. Or the playful but serious tone of her voice when she'd said, "Yet."

Why had she said that if it wasn't true?

His fury then focused on Tanner, for doing anything with Brynn after their lunch line conversation. Sure, Ethan had tried to downplay his feelings for Brynn, but Tanner had known. He *did* know Ethan quite well, and had for a long time.

Someone sat next to him, and he barely glanced at them.

"You all alone?" a woman asked, her voice set high on sugar and twang.

"I guess." He looked at her, at her obvious blonde dye-job and her swirling green eyes. She possessed beauty in the lines of her face, the curves of her body. "Are you?"

"At the moment."

"Want to go grab some dinner?" The words left his mouth before he gave them thought.

Her smile widened. "Sure."

"Can you drive?" he asked as he stood up. "I came with a friend." The last word choked his throat, and Ethan coughed to clear it.

"Sure thing, honey. What's your name?"

"Ethan," he said. "Yours?"

"Alyssa."

8

Brynn dropped exhausted into bed each night that week. She'd forgotten how grueling the first week of training could be. Even though she'd spent everyday in the saddle, simply riding around an arena wasn't the same as pushing Washington to take that right turn tighter, or forcing him to go only four inches wide before cutting on the last left turn.

She stood in the shower on Saturday night, her mind wandering from her dismal twenty-second runs down the block to Ethan. She hadn't seen him all week, but then again, she didn't expect to. Their worlds in the rodeo circuit wouldn't overlap until they started touring.

Still, she'd thought they'd been getting along really well. She'd watched for him at the opening meetings, but she never did see him. Her phone had been silent all week, but maybe he simply felt as tired as she did.

After donning her pajamas and settling into bed, she texted him. *Church tomorrow morning? I'll let you drive.*

She added a smiley face emoticon to the message and let her thumb hover over the send button. Something nagged at her. Something that said he had a phone too and knew her number.

Her thumb dropped onto the send button, and her message zipped through cyberspace, only two seconds passing before it said "delivered" beneath the timestamp. Her heart pumped out a double beat and she closed her eyes and let her phone rest on her sternum.

Brynn mentally directed Washington toward the first barrel, refusing to allow him to balk at the right turn. He'd made them countless times before. She wasn't sure why he suddenly always had to go left.

Her phone vibrated her out of her frustrations, and she snapped her eyes open.

Can't, Ethan's message said. Nothing more. Nothing less. No explanation. For some reason, the word felt cold against her retinas. Her chest cavity shrank until her heart felt too big inside it, and she thunked her phone down on her nightstand. She sighed as she plugged it in and set an alarm.

She'd try to get a good two hours of training with Washington before heading to church solo. She drifted along the sea of unconsciousness, the feelings of peace she'd experienced last week during church lulling her into a deep sleep.

Six o'clock came too early, but Brynn walked along the icy trail to the barn. She fed Washington, saddled the stallion, and ran him through a few warm-up routines to get his muscles warm. She dragged the barrels into their traditional triangular formation, but she didn't do a whole run. No, she wanted that first right turn to be perfect before moving on.

Washington seemed to feed on her growing agitation, because after only a half-hour of work, he balked at starting another run completely. Feeling her own temper near the snapping point, Brynn dismounted and took his reins in her fingers. She led him around the arena, letting the soft clomp-clomp of his hooves drive away the imbalance in her mind.

They couldn't afford not to be at their best in San Antonio.

The Wrangler Million Dollar Tour loomed before her, and her father's words kept looping in her mind.

You could be the world champion this year.

He traveled with her, kept track of her times, updated her between runs. She'd been second last year overall in the WPRA world standings despite her overall win, but she could be *the* world champion this year.

What a way to go out, she thought as hope coiled in her chest and struck like a snake, leaving a sting against her ribs.

"Takin' a break?" her dad called from the other end of the arena.

"Ready to go again," she said, swinging herself into the saddle. Beneath her, Washington settled, and she leaned over to pat his neck and whisper in his ear. "Let's show him, boy. Come on now. You know how to turn right."

The horse did better that time, but it still wasn't enough. Daddy coached Brynn on how to hold the reins in a different spot, when to pull them back just a fraction of a second earlier. By the time she needed to go shower, Washington and Brynn had mastered the right turn.

———

SHE DIDN'T SEE ETHAN AT CHURCH, THOUGH PART OF HER HAD assumed he'd be there, despite his text. He didn't seem like the type to miss—had sought her out to ask her where to attend. Another week passed, and Brynn shaved precious seconds off her time. She'd just scored a sixteen-point-two when she decided to quit on Friday night.

She'd been in the saddle all day, if not coaching and training with Washington, then riding another horse to increase her physical and mental stamina. She'd watched a couple hours of tape today too, and Daddy had left the practice facility an hour ago to head home and make dinner.

But Brynn didn't want to go home and eat dinner. Chuck had a date, a text which Brynn had rolled her eyes at earlier that morning. Duke was visiting a client in Cheyenne for the weekend, which left Brynn alone with her father.

Again, she thought of Ethan. As she did, she realized she missed him. Surely he wasn't so busy that he couldn't send her a text every now and then. The nearly two weeks of radio silence set off an alarm that Brynn couldn't quite drown out with positive self-talk.

She passed Washington off to one of the volunteers and headed into the bathroom to wash her hands. She splashed cold water on her face and looked at her dripping reflection in the mirror. Her hair looked like it had been attacked by the Tasmanian Devil, and she had dark circles under her eyes.

She sighed, certainly not in any condition to go out to dinner with Ethan, and headed toward the bathroom's exit. Alyssa nearly plowed into her as she came through the swinging door.

"Oh, sorry!" Brynn threw up both hands to shield her face from the door.

"Brynn! Sorry." Alyssa sidestepped and ducked around Brynn. "You headed home?"

"Yeah." She exhaled, the weight of her exhaustion heavy in the sound. "You?"

Alyssa swept her fingers through her flawless hair, which didn't seem to have a single tangle in it. "No, I have a date." Her green eyes sparkled with mischief.

Brynn didn't want to know. "Oh, fun. Have a good time."

"I intend to." She turned from her primping in the mirror. "Do you know Ethan Greene?"

"Ethan Greene?" Brynn's voice caught between her vocal chords and her tongue.

"Yeah, someone said you knew him. We're goin' to the Wild Boar tonight."

The Wild Boar. A rowdy cowboy hangout Brynn wouldn't be

caught dead visiting. "That's...great," she managed to say. "I don't know Ethan that well." She pushed her way out of the bathroom, the pressure of her words nearly causing her own eardrums to burst.

She obviously didn't know Ethan at all if he'd held her hand one week and then started dating Brynn's biggest competitor the next.

Her eyes burned as she left the building. Her long legs ate the distance to her SUV quickly, but she barely made it behind closed doors before a single tear ran down her cheek.

ETHAN SAT ON THE COUCH IN HIS COTTAGE, UTTERLY BORED OUT OF his mind. The last two weeks had been challenging, to say the least. Fighting with himself to stay away from Brynn. Employing his detective skills to figure out her schedule and watch her from darkened doorways. Dodging Alyssa's attempts to talk to him every blasted day. Keeping himself from punching Tanner in the nose every time he offered advice for how to get the horns roped faster.

He had improved in his roping and riding over the past several days. Tanner had even said so. But Ethan didn't need praise. He needed someone he could talk to, someone he could trust.

He'd been hoping that person would be Brynn. For all of three seconds, he thought it might be Alyssa, but after only fifteen minutes with her, he'd regretted his invitation to take her to dinner. All she'd given him was a massive headache. And now, apparently, as he'd watched her pass by the door leading to the roping facility three times before coming in, a stalker.

He'd escaped as fast as he could and taken a dozen wrong turns before he ended up in his garage. He wouldn't put it past the woman to follow him home. Only Brynn knew where he lived, and since Alyssa hadn't shown up yet, Ethan could only assume Brynn hadn't told her.

Brynn.

His heart twisted in his chest. He'd wanted to text her every night. Better, call her, hear her pretty voice over the line. But he hadn't. He'd even gone so far as to take the battery out of his phone one night when the urge to speak with her had reached epic proportions.

He missed her. He marveled how he barely knew her, and yet he missed her. He hadn't missed his mother like this when he'd left home. The only thing that even remotely came close was the longing he felt for Three Rivers Ranch, and that still paled in comparison to the loneliness enveloping him now, without Brynn.

Maybe just call her, he thought.

Don't you dare, the rational side of his brain said. *She kissed another man!*

It wasn't a kiss. She didn't really do anything.

It takes two to tango.

Didn't really see any tangoing.

He'd been going back and forth with himself for almost two solid weeks. He was exhausted. He leaned his head back against the couch and closed his eyes.

Just call her.

Before he could talk himself out of it, he leaned forward and picked up his phone. He pressed call on her name without thinking. Just an action. Something to be done.

"Ethan?" Her voice came through the line as a screech, not the soothing tone he'd been expecting.

"Brynn." Her name tasted like honey on his tongue. Too bad he didn't have anything else to say.

"What do you want?" She bit the words out, and Ethan recoiled from the venom in them.

You, he wanted to say, but he knew that word would push her further away.

"Um...just wanted to see how you were doing. Haven't talked for a while."

"I don't really want to talk to you, Ethan."

He frowned as confusion collected in his veins. "Why not?"

"Why not? Why not?!" She exhaled angrily. "If you don't know, I'm not going to fill you in." She hung up, leaving Ethan to look at his cell like it had mysteriously turned into a deadly spider.

He'd obviously done something wrong, but he couldn't fathom what—besides the nearly two weeks of silence. Fine, that could be it. But would silence really make her so poisonous?

He cursed himself and his foolish pride as he got up and began pacing. What should he do? Confront her about Tanner? Call her back and beg her to tell him what he'd done wrong so he could fix it?

He ground his teeth together. Just like a woman to blame him for something he didn't even know he'd done!

Ethan snatched his phone off the couch and dialed. Tanner, though, not Brynn.

"Hey." The noise coming through the line indicated Tanner had gone to the loudest nightclub in town for dinner.

"Hey, it's Ethan. You gotta second?"

"Sure." The background music quieted. "Just a sec." The line turned silent. "Okay, go."

"So something's up with...." He couldn't say her name. He didn't want to endure Tanner's teasing.

"Brynn," he finally forced himself to say. "I'm worried about her. She won't call me back or anything." Not entirely true, but not entirely false either.

"Maybe that's because you went out with Alyssa."

"Alyssa? What's she got to do with anything? And—" Ethan jabbed his finger into empty air. "That wasn't a date."

"Well, everyone thinks it was."

"Why would they think that?"

"Because that's what she's tellin' everyone."

Ethan pressed his eyes closed and prayed for strength. "It was mac and cheese at a fast-casual place. She paid for herself. Less than an hour. And trust me, that was fifty-nine minutes too long."

Tanner laughed, a full-on roar. "I could've told you that."

Ethan lifted his chin, though he remained in his empty cottage. "Tell me about you and Brynn, then."

"Nothin' to tell."

"Right," Ethan scoffed. "I saw you guys a couple of weeks ago. You...looked more than friendly."

Tanner chuckled again. "I've tried things with her. Didn't work out."

"Why'd she drive all the way to Texas to convince me to join the rodeo? Why'd you need to get some keys from her?"

"You should ask her."

"She won't talk to me!"

"Brynn is a feisty little thing," Tanner said. "I'd start my apology with Dove dark chocolate." He gave a final chuckle. "Good luck, cowboy."

Ethan practically punched the end button on his phone, already calculating how long it would take him to get to the grocery store and buy chocolate before he could get over to Brynn's.

9

Brynn ignored the pounding on the front door and headed down the hall to her bedroom. She thought she knew who it would be, and sure enough, a few minutes later Daddy showed up in her doorway. "Ethan's here to see you."

"I don't want to talk to him right now." Brynn managed to keep the raw emotion from her voice, only allowing her anger to surface.

"Why not?"

"Because."

"He's holdin' chocolate."

The fight left Brynn's body. "What kind?"

"Your favorite."

"Chuck," she muttered under her breath as she got up and moved into the hall. Sure enough, tall, blond, and handsome Ethan Greene stood in her front room. She leaned against the wall, barely in the room. "What do you want?"

He thrust the bag of chocolates toward her. Dove dark. He'd definitely gotten to Chuck. She didn't make a move to reach for them. As usual, Ethan wore dark jeans, those black cowboy boots, and a leather jacket over his red button-down shirt. She felt underdressed in her yoga pants and oversized sweatshirt.

His eyes still traveled the length of her body before boring into hers. "I want to talk to you," he said. "Five minutes. You can eat all the chocolate you want. I'll even do most of the talking." He settled onto the couch and waited without looking at her.

His patience seemed endless, and after several moments of battling with herself, she finally joined him, miles of empty space between them as she crammed herself into the opposite end of the sofa. She swiped the bag of candy from his hand as he held it toward her.

"I've been informed of my heinous crime," he said, his sapphire eyes sparking with emotion she couldn't name. Could've been anger. Or desire. Or mockery.

The longer she looked at him, the deeper she fell into those eyes. She recognized the attraction burning through his gaze. A current zipped along her skin, making her shiver. She hadn't had a man look at her the way Ethan was now for years.

"I apparently 'went on a date' with Alyssa Shumway. I can assure you that the shared meal—which she paid for hers and I paid for mine—was torture, and I've spent the last two weeks trying to file a restraining order against the relentless woman."

"Yes, and—wait. What?" Brynn gave herself a few seconds to catch up to what he'd said. "Torture?"

"The worst kind." He held out his palm. "I think I deserve one of those chocolates for my pain."

She sat still, numb. "You don't like Alyssa."

He made a sour face. "Not even a little bit. But since she actually hasn't done anything yet, I'm having a hard time gettin' that restraining order." He kicked half a grin in her direction.

She felt herself returning it, the smile growing wider and wider as she realized the full weight of what he'd said.

"I was hopin' you hadn't eaten dinner yet. That maybe you'd let me take you somewhere nice so I can tell you how awful the past two weeks have been without you." He looked at her with such openness, such honesty, that all her walls crumbled.

"I asked you to church," she whispered. "You said no."

"I was stupid," he said. "I'll tell you all about that too." He glanced toward the mouth of the hallway, where surely Daddy was listening out of sight.

Brynn glanced down at her inappropriate-for-nice-dinners attire. "Give me five minutes to change?"

He ducked his head, concealing his eyes beneath that charcoal hat. "Take as long as you want, cowgirl."

She floated from the room, the word *cowgirl* finally not the worst thing she could be called. In fact, when Ethan said it, it almost sounded like an endearment.

—————

Brynn didn't mind the minute pressure Ethan applied to her back as they squeezed into the packed Italian restaurant. She certainly didn't want to wait outside in the cold, though a half dozen heaters lined the sidewalk.

"This isn't exactly quiet," he murmured, his mouth inches from her ear. "Want to go somewhere else?"

"It's okay," she said, turning toward him. She froze when she came within kissing distance. He stalled too, his eyes hooking hers and holding tight. She swallowed, already imagining what his lips would feel like, what the scruff on his face would feel like, where he might place his hands as he kissed her.

He cleared his throat and managed to back up a step. The spell between them broke, and a sting of disappointment at a lost opportunity pricked Brynn's heart. Not that she wanted her first kiss with this handsome man to happen in a busy restaurant.

"I love their beef ravioli here," she said. "We can wait, right? You don't have anything else goin' on?"

"Just sleep," he said, stifling a yawn. "This rodeo thing is more tiring than I remember."

She arched her back, which had developed a kink on the drive over. "Tell me about it."

"You're goin' to San Antonio in a few weeks, right?"

"Yeah, I'm trying to win the Women's world this year."

Admiration crept into his expression. "That's great. What do you think your chances are?"

Brynn groaned inwardly. She didn't want to spend the night with Ethan talking about the rodeo. She hashed everything over so often with Daddy, and she definitely didn't view Ethan as a father figure.

"Don't answer that," he said as a pair of chairs opened up. He gestured her toward them and they sat down, finally able to have more breathing room. "Tell me about your mom instead."

Gratitude filled her. First that he didn't want to talk rodeo either. Then that he'd seen her for more than a cowgirl—again. And third that he'd asked about her mom. So many of the men Brynn went out with avoided the topic, like it was taboo or something she didn't want to talk about.

"She was my best friend," Brynn said. "She loved fashion and jewelry. She taught me all different ways to braid my hair. Once, as an experiment, we braided my hair in a different way for a whole month. Momma always said we should've blogged about it. But we didn't."

Memories crowded into her mind, all of them good, and strong, and happy. "I have a secret." She reached for Ethan's hand and pressed her palm to his. The natural way he enveloped her hand, how comfortable she felt with him, sent a thrill through her at the same time a burst of fear entered her heart.

What about her no-cowboy policy? And what would Ethan do once he found out she was quitting the rodeo circuit? She didn't know where she'd live after she quit, but she knew it wasn't

Colorado Springs. Knew she was ready to move on with her life. Go somewhere else. Be someone different.

Still, she wanted to snuggle into him, inhale the woodsy scent of his skin and find out if his lips felt as soft as they looked.

"A secret?" He settled their joined hands on his thigh. "This I have to hear."

Brynn smiled before inhaling deeply. "Before Momma died, we used to talk all the time about me goin' to beauty school." She didn't know if Daddy knew that. He'd been so busy with his horse boarding program—something Duke had taken over after the move, after her rodeo career exploded.

Ethan's eyebrows disappeared under the brim of his hat. "Beauty school? Huh."

"Yeah. It sounds weird, right? Like it doesn't fit my personality."

"Give me a minute to think about it." He looked into the crowd, then back at her. "I think it fits just fine." He leaned closer and pressed his lips to her temple. Her pulse shot into rapid fire gear, sending out so many beats she felt sure she'd explode.

"I can see why you don't wear a lot of makeup now, or do more than braids with your hair." With his free hand, he lifted one of her braided pigtails and let it drop back to her shoulder. "But I think you're beautiful."

Those captivating eyes sucked at her, drew her deeper into their glorious depths, until she realized she'd moved her face to within kissing distance of his again.

"Ethan, party of two."

Ethan stood, bringing a shell-shocked Brynn with him. Was she really going to kiss him? She'd been trying not to lie to herself, and as they followed the hostess toward a table for two in the back of the restaurant, Brynn admitted that she'd like to kiss Ethan Greene more than just about anything. She tossed a prayer toward the ceiling as he asked her which side she wanted—chair or booth bench?—that an opportunity in an appropriate place would present itself that night. And that she'd be brave enough to take it.

Dinner passed, with easy conversation and delicious food. Surprise, surprise, Ethan ordered the steak and rosemary mashed potatoes, and the fact that Brynn knew what he liked brought her more joy than should be possible.

They drove back to her place in companionable silence, and she again appreciated that she didn't have to be Chatty Kathy around Ethan. She enjoyed his calm, strong demeanor. That he only spoke the words he deemed necessary and not a bunch of talk just to fill the silence. He asked about important things, and genuinely seemed interested in her life.

In short, she'd never met a man like him before. Even Dave, her once-fiancé hadn't treated Brynn so well.

She rode next to him in his truck, her hand secured in his, her head lolling against his shoulder. Her head drooped as sleep tried to claim her, but she jerked awake with an embarrassed giggle.

"I'm more tired than I thought," she said.

"It's pretty late," he said. "You practicing tomorrow?"

"Everyday." She yawned. "I've been getting up early and working with Washington here, because he's decided turning right isn't for him. Well, he does it, but it's still a bit inconsistent."

Ethan chuckled as he turned onto her street. "You'll set him straight."

"Daddy comes out and coaches. We've almost got him there." Nervous energy suddenly filled her bones as he pulled into her driveway. "Then I head over to the official training facilities, and watch tape, and you know." She waved her hand, not wanting to re-live what she spent hours doing everyday.

"I've been out of the rodeo business for six years," he said, cutting the headlights but leaving the engine idling. "I had no idea how much training it takes. And not just with the horse."

"You haven't been out of the saddle, though. Right?"

"I can ride," he said. "But I normally don't run or do sit-ups.

I've got this insane trainer, and he makes me workout every day. Says I need more strength in my core." He groaned. "Don't tell him about the mashed potatoes I ate tonight."

She laughed, using the motion to slide the teensiest bit closer to him. "I'm sure your core is plenty strong."

"Not according to Weston."

"Looks great to me."

The resulting silence repeated her words back to her over and over again.

"So you think I'm pretty handsome, then. Is that it?" He released her hand and lifted his arm over her shoulders, drawing her closer to him and enveloping her in a cloud of his manly scent.

"A little," she admitted. "I mean, you're not bad—for a cowboy."

He stiffened, and so did she. Despair poured through her. Instead of seizing the moment God had given her with Ethan, she'd ruined it. "Walk me to the door?" She whispered so her voice wouldn't betray her misery.

"Sure." He slid out of the truck and helped her down behind him. "Thank you for lettin' me talk to you, and then take you to dinner." He captured her hand in his as they moved up the sidewalk to her front porch.

She paused in the halo of light from the overhead fixture. Was she really going to kiss him on her front porch? She'd done that in high school in Texas, before she'd moved here and finished her education with tutors.

Every nerve in her body wanted to kiss him, and kiss him now. She tilted her head back, and he leaned down. His hands snaked around her waist, drawing her body almost flush against his.

"Brynn," he whispered, not quite a question and not quite a statement.

She imagined him to be asking her permission to kiss

her. "Yeah?"

The door behind her squealed as it opened. Brynn leapt out of Ethan's arms and glared at Chuck as he filled the doorway. "There you are. I've been callin' you all night."

Annoyance sang through her soul. "If it were important, Chuck, I would've answered."

"It is important, Brynn." He glanced at Ethan, as if just now noticing he stood there. "Oh, hey, Ethan."

The man Brynn desperately wanted to kiss nodded at her brother and took a step backward, into the shadows. Her second chance that night had been stolen from her. She wanted to hit something—preferably Chuck.

"What's so important, Chuck?"

"Duke was unloading Washington tonight, after your practice, and the horse stumbled. He's got a limp."

The air left Brynn's lungs. The world narrowed to just the porch light shining on her. Chuck said something else. Ethan did too. She stepped into the house and someone helped her sit on the couch.

Everything came rushing back then, and life seemed to whir and whir and whir. It was Ethan who finally said, "It'll be okay, Brynn. It's just rodeo."

It's just rodeo.

The words looped in her mind as she went with Chuck out to the barn to see Washington. As she got ready for bed once she'd been assured the horse was alive and as comfortable as Duke could make him. As she drifted into sleep, she felt and finally understood the weight of Ethan's statement.

It's just rodeo. No one's died. Everything will be okay.

It's just rodeo.

———

SOMETHING STILL WASN'T QUITE RIGHT WITH BRYNN WHEN ETHAN

talked to her on Saturday evening after he finished training. She claimed to be fine, that Washington had been running that afternoon, that she felt confident they'd still be able to race in San Antonio in a few weeks.

He believed her on all that. But he also believed she had more to her than rodeo. Her admission that she wanted to go to beauty school—okay, she hadn't said those exact words—had unsettled him.

Hope flared every time he thought of her leaving the rodeo circuit. He had a feeling she didn't want to be here any more than he did. But she was afraid to leave. Why, he didn't know. He'd looked her up—she'd made upwards of two hundred thousand dollars last year. She could afford to retire, travel the world, go to beauty school, do whatever she wanted.

He pushed her from his mind long enough to doze on the couch, having slept poorly the night before. Even now, his body hummed with repressed energy, from the kisses he hadn't been able to have.

A text came through, and Ethan jolted out of his catnap, his heart beating heavily in his chest. He fumbled for his phone, hoping it wasn't his mother, asking him to come to Sunday dinner again. He'd turned her down twice, and he didn't have the gumption to do it again.

Church tomorrow?

Brynn's invitation made him smile.

You never did explain why you said no last week.

He hadn't. He didn't want her to know how petty and jealous he'd been. Of Tanner, no less. How distrusting of her.

Church tomorrow sounds great, he thumbed out. *You up to go to lunch at my mom's afterward?*

She hadn't invited him yet, but Ethan figured he should ask her first this time. He didn't want her to think she'd never get to see him when he only lived ten minutes away. He sent her a text while he waited for Brynn to answer.

Sure, came her reply at the same time his mom sent, *Sounds great. How does 1:30 sound?*

1:30 okay? he sent to Brynn while confirming with his mom that the time would work. Church ended at eleven-thirty, but he could think of several things he and Brynn could do in the interim hours.

We can come back to my place after church, he texted. *Take a nap or whatever. Trust me, to deal with my mom, you'll need one.*

Brynn confirmed, and Ethan felt like the stars had aligned.

Sunday morning dawned with Ethan still lounging in bed. He'd been awake for a while, but had determined not to get out of bed until the sun rose. Lightning danced in his stomach as he thought about the day ahead. Church with Brynn. Time alone with Brynn. Lunch at his mom's with Brynn.

Hopefully, he could figure out how to kiss Brynn during all that.

He showered, and ate a banana and a protein bar—courtesy of his physical trainer—and decided to check out his social media networks. He didn't care much to keep in touch with anyone whose phone number he didn't already have, but he opened his laptop and logged into Facebook anyway.

A slew of notifications came up, as he hadn't been on the site in at least a month. He ignored them and searched for Brynn Bowman. She had a fanpage with almost forty thousand fans, and a personal profile. He requested to be friends with her and navigated to the dog shelter website.

He'd still been thinking about getting a dog, but his enthusiasm for the pup had waned, due to his long training hours. And in a few weeks, he'd be on the road. He closed the browser tab, knowing it just wasn't the right time to get a dog.

His disappointment was dulled by Brynn's friend acceptance. Immediately after that notification, he saw that today was her birthday.

Ice ran through his veins. Today was her birthday? Was that really true?

He couldn't miss her birthday, not when they were just getting things started. But she hadn't told him.

Doesn't matter, he told himself. *You don't miss a woman's birthday, no matter what.*

Agreed.

For once, both sides of himself had concurred. He glanced around his cottage, desperate for the perfect gift to materialize, already wrapped.

Of course it didn't. One glance at the clock told him Brynn would be waiting at the curb in thirty minutes. That didn't leave him much time to run to the store—and besides dark chocolate, he didn't even know what to get her.

He couldn't call Tanner and ask. Too obvious.

He didn't have either of her brother's numbers.

Once she arrived, he'd be spending the rest of the day with her. What could he do in only thirty minutes?

Twenty-nine minutes.

Twenty-eight minutes.

Ethan's panic reared into a tidal wave that splashed against his insides.

Get it together, he commanded himself.

He took a deep breath and got online. She'd said she and her mother used to talk about cosmetology school, and his memory sparked with the knowledge that she'd named her horse after a teacher who owned a salon. He could search the web with the best of them, and twenty-four minutes later, he had a virtual gift card for a spa pedicure at the ritziest place in Colorado Springs. Now all he had to do was find a printer, or ask Brynn for her email address so he could forward the confirmation number to her.

Knocking sounded on the door and Ethan slammed his laptop closed, his confidence soaring toward the skies.

"Hey," he said when he opened the door and found Brynn on his doorstep. He swept her into a hug, hoping the embrace wasn't moving forward too fast. But hugging usually came before kissing, right?

She melted into his arms, and he forced himself to pull back. "You ready?"

"Ready." She smiled. "You weren't waiting on the curb."

"I had some things to get done before church. I was on my way out." He followed her out and locked the door behind him. They held hands on the way to church, and during the service. Ethan's anxiety skyrocketed when the sermon ended and they made their way back to the parking lot, and then his house. Brynn didn't seem nervous, or worried, or afraid.

Why was he? He'd kissed women before. But only the type who went for his ultra-forward approach. Not someone like Brynn, where he'd taken more time, learned things about her beyond her physical appearance, appreciated who she was and who he could be with her.

His mind spun and he didn't get out of her SUV until she came around the passenger side and knocked on the window. He jumped and fumbled for the handle.

"Sorry," he said as he spilled from the car. "Just thinkin' about something."

"What the pastor said?" Brynn linked her arm through his as they navigated around the garage.

"What did you like about what he said?" Ethan asked, because he hadn't heard a single thing. Not with her vanilla perfume clouding his senses and her soft skin touching his.

"Oh, you know. The usual."

Ethan grinned. She hadn't been listening either. The idea gave him courage, and as he unlocked the door, he wondered how he could kiss her without coming on too strong.

They entered his house and shut out the winter wind behind them. "Tea?" he asked.

"Do you have hot chocolate?"

"Sure," he said. "And I even know how to make it." He poured milk into two mugs and stuck them in the microwave. "My mom's a pretty good cook," he said to make conversation. "But if you're hungry now, you can look in the fridge."

She entered the kitchen, bringing her intoxicating scent with her and opened the fridge. She peered inside for a few minutes before saying, "You're so organized."

"I'm not home that much. Empty doesn't mean organized."

"These yogurts are sorted by color."

"That's not true." He joined her and looked inside his fridge, where the seven flavors of yogurt he'd bought yesterday—at his trainer's insistence—were sitting in color groups. "Well, that was an accident." A flush crept up his neck.

"Yeah, I don't think so," she teased.

"Go look in my closet." He turned back to the microwave and reached for the first mug.

"You want me to go in your bedroom?"

He froze halfway through ripping open the hot chocolate packet. Forcing himself to chuckle, he said, "Yeah, better not do that."

"I'll bet it's immaculate."

"You'd be disappointed."

"I doubt it."

He abandoned the hot chocolate and turned around to face her. "I'm not perfect," he said.

"I know that." She grinned. "After all, you went to dinner with Alyssa Shumway."

He didn't know if he should laugh or defend himself again. He didn't want to tell her the real reason he'd been so blind to Alyssa's obvious flaws. He managed to match her smile with one of his own, but he twisted back to the counter where the hot chocolate waited.

After he finished making their drinks, he handed her one and took his into the living room, where he settled on the sofa. "You wanna watch a movie or something?"

She could've chosen to sit on the other end of the couch or in the armchair beside it. Instead, she snuggled right into him, resting her head against his chest as he lifted his arm to drape across her shoulders.

"I might fall asleep," she warned.

"That's okay." His voice sounded like he'd swallowed frogs. "I told you my mother requires one to be at their full attention."

She giggled, and the sound drove him toward the edge of reason. He set his mug down on the side table and deliberately reached for hers.

She gave it to him, but she didn't turn to look at him. The moment hadn't arrived. He wondered if it ever would. He reached for the remote and selected a movie from the cable menu. "This okay?" he asked about the romantic comedy he'd chosen.

"I've never seen it."

"You probably don't watch many movies."

"I can't believe you do."

"I don't. I've just happened to see this one."

She tilted her head back and grinned at him. "Right. 'Happened' to see a chick flick? Must've been on a date or something."

Seizing the opportunity, he swept his free hand down the side of her face, along her neck. He watched the sizzle in her eyes deepen into dark pools of desire. She licked her lips, and Ethan couldn't tear his eyes from her mouth.

"Brynn," he said, the same way he had last night. Except, here, now, there wasn't anyone to interrupt them. "I happen to like romantic movies." He inched closer, so close her breath drifted across his chin.

"Uh huh," she said, her eyes falling closed. Ethan leaned down, the moment finally right.

10

An eternity passed before Ethan's lips met Brynn's. She turned further into him, sliding one arm around his back. Everything inside her sighed at the sweet, chocolatey taste of his mouth, the gentle pressure of his lips against hers.

He deepened the kiss, and Brynn's hunger for him multiplied. She matched his slow pace, unwilling to show him how much he affected her. She felt herself falling, felt his warm hands catch her, felt such a strong sense of safety with him.

His kiss didn't remind her of any of her previous encounters with cowboys. Tanner's had been rough and demanding. Dave's a bit limp.

But the way Ethan kissed her, she felt cherished. Valued. She wanted to feel this way, be kissed by him, everyday of her life.

She pushed away the fear, the doubts, the uncertainty of the future, and just focused on kissing the cowboy she enjoyed spending time with.

Eventually, he pulled back. "Wow," he whispered, tracing his thumb over her bottom lip. He touched his mouth to her temple, the tip of her nose, and came back to her mouth for a second kiss.

Wow didn't even begin to cover it.

T REPIDATION TUMBLED THROUGH B RYNN AS SHE FOLLOWED E THAN up the front steps to his mother's front door. She gripped his fingers with a ferocity that made him turn before he entered the house.

"It's okay," he said. "She's nice enough."

"I haven't met anyone's mother in a long time." That, plus the fact that she was meeting his mother so early in their relationship, sent fear straight through her.

He leaned down and skated his lips across hers, a ghost of a touch, there but gone so quickly, she ached for more. A tease. Sure enough, when she opened her eyes, she found him grinning at her like the Cheshire Cat.

"What?" she asked, a rush of embarrassment striking her at how easily she succumbed to his charms.

"I like that I can kiss you whenever I want." He squeezed her fingers. "But I got you somethin' else for your birthday too. You'll have to wait until after lunch, though."

Surprise mingled with pleasure inside her mind. "How did you know it was my birthday? Chuck told you, didn't he? He's got to stop meddling—"

Ethan inched closer again, rendering her silent. And breathless, though he didn't need to know that. She forced herself to exhale and take a slow breath. A mistake, as she got a noseful of his dreamy scent and chocolatey lips.

"I haven't talked to Chuck," Ethan said. "Not even once."

"How did—the chocolates, and my birthday."

Ethan ducked his head, using that blasted cowboy hat to shield his eyes. "Tanner told me about the chocolate. Facebook alerted me to your birthday." He lifted his chin and grinned. "But now I know where to go should I need to know anything else about you." He chuckled and turned back to the door. "You ready?"

"Ready as I'll ever be."

He opened the screen door and then the front door, calling to his mom as he entered. They went up the few steps in the split-level house to the kitchen, where she greeted them wearing an apron over her clothes.

"Ethan." She reached out and embraced him, and Brynn found the sight of the tall, muscled cowboy bending down to hug his shorter, rounder mother endearing. She wore a smile when Mrs. Greene turned her attention to Brynn.

"Hello," Brynn said. "I'm—"

His mother put both hands over her heart. "Brynn Bowman."

Brynn's chest cavity collapsed, but she kept her grin hitched in place. "Nice to meet you, ma'am."

"You didn't tell me you were bringin' home Brynn Bowman." Ethan's mother swatted at Ethan's bicep and started patting her hair. "Oh, my. A celebrity, right here in my house."

Ethan glanced at Brynn, his expression unreadable. She was sure hers was too. Whenever she got recognized in public—which happened more often than she liked—she disappeared behind her championship mask. She just didn't want to do it now, with his mother. Or with him, ever.

"Mom, she's just a girl."

Ethan's words stung, though Brynn understood why he'd said them.

"I used to win rodeos too." He moved into the kitchen and pulled two bottles of water from the fridge. "I was even a champion. A celebrity."

His mother acted like she hadn't even heard him. Brynn accepted the water bottle and allowed Ethan to corral her into the living room. "Sorry," he whispered as he sat next to her on the couch. "I didn't know she'd react like this."

Brynn nodded like it was fine, but she now understood why

Ethan said she should take a nap before spending time with his mother.

By the time they ate and could leave without seeming rude, Brynn's kindness meter had dropped to empty. Since she'd spent so much time pretending to enjoy everything around her—though, to be fair, the chicken fried steak was delicious—she didn't have time to obsess over whether a relationship with Ethan was smart.

She'd looked at cosmetology schools online last night, as well as this morning. She originally thought she didn't much care where she went, but after doing a little research, she'd decided on the Regency Beauty College, which had locations all over the country—including two in Colorado.

But she didn't want to stay in the state. Regency had campuses everywhere, including sunny California and tropical Florida. Brynn wanted to get away from everything rodeo and see if she could find herself.

The problem had become Ethan. Last night and this morning, she'd reasoned that he was just a friend. A friend that ignited strong passions inside her, sure. But just a friend.

The kiss in his cottage had changed everything.

"You okay?" Ethan asked as he pulled into his garage and cut the engine. "You're awfully quiet."

"Just thinking," she said. "And relaxing after that tense lunch."

He chuckled, but it held a nervous edge. "Sorry I didn't properly warn you. I tried."

She tossed him a baleful glare. "You could've tried harder."

His grin turned predatory and he swept his arms around her, pinning her against his very solid chest. "Sorry." He didn't sound too apologetic, but Brynn didn't care much once he placed his cowboy hat on the dashboard and kissed the spot just behind her jaw.

"Yeah, really sounds like it." Her words came out like clouds, airy and barely there.

"I really am." He brushed his lips up to her earlobe, and then to her mouth. After the shortest kiss in history, he pulled back. "You gonna be mad all afternoon?"

The wicked twinkle in his eye suggested that he knew he'd won her over with his affections. She pushed against his chest at the same time she giggled. "Let me go."

He held her fast. "Not until you promise me you're not mad." He kissed her forehead, the corner of each eye, and just below her chin. She sucked in a breath and wrapped her arms around his neck, her fingers wandering up into his hair.

"Promise me, Brynn." He hovered half an inch from her mouth. "I don't want you to be mad on your birthday."

She trembled with the desire to kiss him. Close as he was, he couldn't stop her. She closed the distance between them, pressing herself even further into him, and kissed him like she'd never kissed a man before.

ETHAN ADORED THE WAY BRYNN'S MOUTH MOLDED TO HIS. HE loved that she kissed him first. Enjoyed holding her, and talking to her, and spending time with her. He also knew things could get complicated really quickly.

He pulled away, his breathing ragged and his body screaming at him to kiss her again. But his mind warned him to *slow down. Slow down now, cowboy.*

He took a calming breath and leaned his forehead against hers. "Happy birthday," he whispered, wishing he'd be in Colorado next year to celebrate with her. But he wouldn't be, and he knew it.

She should know it too, whispered through his mind.

Later, he told himself. *I'm not going to ruin her birthday.*

Plus, they'd only kissed a few times. He'd only known her for a few weeks. The beginning stages of a relationship were always the most exciting, and while Ethan would never hurt Brynn intentionally, he also knew they could breakup at any time, for any reason. He just didn't want the reason to be him leaving the rodeo circuit.

"Should we go in?" he asked. "It's starting to get cold out here."

She nodded and he opened the truck door and got out. They held hands on the way into his cottage, where he couldn't wait any longer to give her the gift he'd purchased.

"Okay." He released her hand and backed away from her. "I just found out it was your birthday this mornin', and I didn't have time to go to the store. So...." He pulled out his phone, giddiness combining with worry. What if pedicures had become part of her past? What if they conjured painful memories of her mother?

"I just need your email address, and then I can send you the —well, you'll see."

She cocked one hip and appraised him. "Is this some ploy to get my email address?"

"I already know where you live," he shot back. "And you've been kissin' me all day. I think me havin' your email address is tolerable."

"*You've* been kissin' me," she argued.

"I didn't hear any complaining."

A beautiful blush stained her cheeks, which brought a great deal of satisfaction to Ethan. "So?"

"What'd you get me?"

"I want it to be a surprise." He couldn't believe she was being this difficult about an email address. "All right, then. You'll have to wait until I can get to a printer."

She tossed her head back and laughed, her loose hair cascading over her shoulders. "You're too easy."

He growled through a smile and strode toward her. She

shrieked and scampered into the kitchen. But there was no exit there. He stalked closer to her, cornering her next to the sink. "Are you gonna tell me or not?"

She giggled as his hands encircled her waist, and a delightful thrill shot down his back when her hands slid up his chest. "Okay, okay," she conceded. "I'll give you my email address."

He backed away, ready to forward the gift certificate to her. She pulled out her phone as she dictated the email address, and Ethan held his breath as he finished and sent the email.

He knew the moment she got it. Her eyes flitted from side to side as she read it, realized what it was, and sucked in a breath.

"Ethan."

"Okay?"

She looked at him, her eyes storming with emotion. She lifted her chin, an edge in her expression that didn't speak of happiness. "Do you know what Daddy gave me?"

"No." He hoped it wasn't a spa pedicure.

"A rope."

Ethan frowned. Her father hadn't seemed overly fond of ropers. "Like...a rope? What—?"

"So I can start learning to calf rope."

"But there aren't roping events for women in the rodeo."

"There are in women-only rodeos."

Ethan heard the disdain in her voice, saw the quiver in her chin. He stepped closer to her, ready to lend her his strength. "Have you told your father you don't want to rope?"

She shrugged, the motion releasing a single tear. She wiped it away before he could.

"Why don't you tell him?"

"He's taken care of everything for me in the rodeo circuit," she said.

"Yeah. But—"

"We have a delicate relationship." She turned away, slipped

past him, and sat on his couch. "Thank you for the gift certificate. It's perfect." Her voice cracked on the last word.

Ethan hurried to sit next to her. "I thought you'd like a pedicure."

She threw her arms around him and held on tight. "I'd love a pedicure."

"I'm sorry it upset you."

"I'm not really upset."

"You're crying."

"Only because it's the nicest thing I've gotten for my birthday since Momma died."

Ethan's heart ached that her brothers and father hadn't been more in tune with what Brynn wanted and needed in her life. He wanted to be the one to give her the perfect gift every year for her birthday.

"Brynn, I have a confession," he said, though it was her birthday. The rational side of him had won.

She pulled away from him and wiped her face. She sniffled and took a deep breath. "Okay, I'm ready for it."

"I'm not going to be in Colorado Springs very long."

Panic raced through her eyes. "How long?"

"I'm only doing a favor for Tanner. I'm not joining the rodeo circuit permanently."

Her shoulders settled and her expression turned into one of resignation. "You'll go back to Texas."

He felt like he needed to defend himself, his choices, his likes. "I love ranching," he said. "I love Three Rivers." He paused, knowing he didn't love Brynn—yet. He wondered if he could, given enough time. He thought so. Either way, it was way too early to tell her that.

"I don't love bull riding or roping."

"I know how you feel." She worried her bottom lip between her teeth, her eyes suddenly looking everywhere but at him. "You'll stay through the circuit, though, right?"

"Yeah." He exhaled. "If we do well enough, I'll stay in the circuit all the way through the finals in December."

"That's a whole year," she said.

"I just wanted you to know," he said. "What with the travel starting soon and all that. You should know I'm not planning on sticking around after this season."

She nodded and slid her hands into his. "Thanks for letting me know." She leaned forward like she wanted to kiss him.

"I wanted you to know," he murmured as she continued to inch forward. "Because I'm not real sure where this can go if I'm plannin' on leaving."

"It's a year away," she said, the edges of her lips catching his. "You worry too much." She pressed a kiss against his mouth.

He put a knuckle of space between them. "I don't want to hurt you."

"Let's just see what happens."

"Really?" He searched her face for a hint of a lie, but found none.

"Sure. I'm interested in seeing what happens." She pulled back a bit more. "Aren't you?"

He cradled her face in his hands. "Definitely." He brought her closer so he could kiss her again.

11

Brynn traveled to San Antonio with her father and Chuck, with Washington in the trailer behind them. As the miles passed, she ran through the bracket, where she needed to place in the top four out of ten to advance. She thought through the semi-finals, where she needed to be in the top five out of twenty. She envisioned herself winning the whole rodeo, doing all of her runs in fourteen seconds or less.

Washington had healed just fine, and he hadn't balked at a right turn in several days. She'd managed to get all their practice runs under fourteen-point-four seconds.

You've got this, she told herself.

Alyssa Shumway was going to San Antonio too—a lot of cowgirls would be there. Brynn put the competition from her mind as they pulled into the parking lot at her practice farm. She'd let Daddy take care of everything, the way he always did. She'd focus on Washington and herself, the way she always did.

She kept her headphones securely in place as she got Washington out of the trailer. Chuck greeted their old friends, the MacDonald's, who always hosted several cowgirls during the San Antonio Stock Show and Rodeo, as they couldn't practice on-site.

Her bracket didn't begin for two more days, but Brynn always arrived this early. Daddy took care of the trailer while she saddled and got Washington into a walk. In a couple of days, he'd be acclimated to the weather here—so different from Colorado in February. They'd have practiced their run a hundred times.

We'll be ready, Brynn thought.

Two days later, she lined up at the rodeo grounds after she'd drawn to go first in the bracket, and in the few seconds before she was set to go, the crowd noise and announcer's voice fell into her deaf ears. The faces blurred. She could only see barrels, the exact track she needed to guide Washington along. She hadn't watched a single ride before this one, though the first bracket had started three days ago. She'd ignored the tapes Daddy had brought her, having watched hundreds of hours of footage over the past month.

The judge signaled her, and Washington shot forward. She urged him on, her legs bouncing against his sides, barely pulling on the rein that would direct him right. He took the turn perfectly, already sprinting toward the next barrel in the triangle.

Her braid bounced against her back. The smell of the dirt and horse met her nose. Washington rounded the next barrel, and Brynn held herself straight up as the horse nearly went horizontal.

"Last one," she muttered as Washington veered the tiniest bit right before cutting the corner so close, she thought he'd surely tip the barrel. She brought her knee as close to his body as possible—while keeping the reins tight and her back straight, like Daddy had coached her—to avoid the barrel.

Washington raced toward the finish line, into the tunnel, and finally slowed as she directed him around the bend and behind the scenes. She leaned over and patted his heaving neck. "Nice job, Wash."

Her own heart and breathing labored, as if she'd run the pattern around the triangular barrels. She had no idea what her time was. Daddy charted all of that. She'd asked him not to tell her any of the times, any of the standings, nothing. She didn't want to know. She was stressed enough as it was.

She dismounted as Ethan rounded the corner into the holding pens. "Whoa," he said. "That was absolutely amazing." He swept her into a hug that lifted her feet off the ground. All her cares and worries seemed to evaporate inside the safety of his arms.

He set her down and gave her a quick kiss. "You are the fastest—"

"I don't want to know."

His expression turned puzzled. "You don't want to know how you stand?"

"No. Daddy takes care of all of it. I just race." She flashed him a smile so he'd know she wasn't upset.

"I don't understand."

His confusion was cute. She laughed and slipped her hand into his. "I race. That's it. I don't worry about the clock or the other riders. I worry about my form, and Washington's performance. That's it."

"So you don't know you just—"

"If you keep talking, I might have to slug you." She tossed him a wicked grin.

He stared at her for another few seconds, then broke into laughter. "I've never met anyone who doesn't know what their times are. Who doesn't want to know where they stand."

"Glad I can amuse you."

"Oh, come on." He swept one arm around her waist and drew her into his side.

She stretched up on her toes and kissed his cheek. "Thanks for comin' to watch. Now go sit in the stands and marvel at my amazingness. I'm going to go take care of Washington and await the results."

He chuckled, twisting into her and giving her a proper kiss before leaving her to her mental focus and her horse.

After the other contestants had ridden, Brynn followed the rodeo volunteer down the path that led back to the arena, her hopes hovering somewhere near the ceiling of the indoor facility. She felt like she and Washington had been on the dirt for mere breaths, hardly enough time to even count. Surely she'd qualified for the semi-finals.

She steadfastly refused to look up to the board to see who had already advanced from bracket one and who was coming up in brackets three, four, and five. Right now, all that mattered was bracket two. The announcer came over the loudspeaker, and the crowd quieted.

He started with tenth place, though only the top four would move on to the semi-finals. Brackets three, four, and five would produce an additional twelve riders for the semis. Only five of the twenty would make it into the final round from each semi-final, and then Brynn just had to be the best of ten.

She clapped from the back of her horse, thrilled when her name wasn't called for fifth, fourth, or third. She could maybe win. Washington had been flawless tonight.

Her name wasn't called as second, and the crowd went wild, because they knew who the winner was. She swore she heard the deep bellow that belonged to Ethan, but she didn't look. Didn't smile. Did nothing.

"And your first place winner from bracket two is...the current WPRA World leader, Brynn Bowman!"

Relief and happiness poured through her in giant waves. Her most diplomatic and joyful smile sprang to her face. She lifted her hand to wave to the crowd, stepping forward and then back.

And just like that, the second bracket ended. She followed the other riders out of the arena, her mind already on tomorrow, when Ethan would rope in bracket three. Once inside the tunnel, away from the crowd and the next event, Alyssa caught her eye, glared at her as she passed, and Brynn actually felt sorry for her. She had too much time to worry about other people, something Daddy had taught Brynn not to do. A rush of gratitude for her father filled her. She needed to tell him thank you once in a while. He'd trained her to be an iron-minded cowgirl, and she'd been second in earnings last year. If she could be first this year, she'd win the World Championship.

With her bracket over, she got Washington fed and brushed down and in the trailer. She changed out of her racing clothes and put on a clean pair of jeans and a dark red tank top. Here in Texas, she could wear such things. She let her hair down and re-donned her hat.

When she finished, Ethan and Chuck waited for her in the contestant's tent. Ethan hugged her again before releasing her to Chuck's embrace.

"Where's Daddy?" she asked.

"He wasn't feeling well," Chuck said. "He left right after you won."

Brynn catalogued the information. Daddy never got sick, but she pushed away the worry when Ethan captured her hand in his. "You ready?"

"Yep." She turned to Chuck. "We're goin' to dinner. You want to come?"

He took in their joined hands and shook his head. "No, you guys go on ahead. I'll see you back at the house."

Brynn nodded and left the brightly lit tent in favor of the dark night—and time alone with Ethan.

ETHAN DROVE TO THE OUTSKIRTS OF THE CITY, ABOUT AS FAR FROM the rodeo arena as he could go. Brynn hadn't said as much, but he knew she wouldn't want to eat in any of the restaurants close by, where she could be recognized and congratulated for her amazing win.

"So can we talk about your times now?" he asked. His admiration for her had only grown when he watched her ride. The woman was flawless, every elbow, knee, and finger in the exact right spot. Her tawny hat and navy, long-sleeved shirt with sponsor patches complimented her midnight hair.

Of course, he liked the slim cut of the tank top she now wore too. He reached over and took her hand. "You know you ran under fourteen seconds, right?"

"I do now," she said. "But Daddy usually tells me in the tent afterward."

"He said he had a headache," Ethan said, picking up on the worried undertone of her voice. "I told him I'd take care of you and bring you home."

She smiled warmly at him, and he brought her hand to his lips. "You really were amazing. I mean, I've seen barrel racing before, but that was magical."

"How did your practice session go?"

"Great," he said, his mind flashing back to that afternoon's time in the arena with Tanner. "I got the horns the first time, every time, so that's good. I could've dallied and turned faster, but I'll be ready tomorrow."

Ethan didn't let her know how nervous he was about the competition. He wanted to get to the semis and then the finals. He felt like he had a lot to prove—to Tanner, to the other cowboys, to himself.

"I need to break out of the box faster too," he said, more to himself than to her.

"Mmm."

He switched his mind off from rodeo, though he wanted to tell her that they'd completed their last practice run in only six-point-two seconds.

Tomorrow, they were slated to rope fourth in the bracket, and

Ethan didn't want his inconsistencies or failures to keep Tanner from defending his championship. He let the doubts swing from one side of his head to the other, banishing them completely when he pulled into one of a row of steakhouses.

"We can just get take-out and go home," he whispered when he found Brynn's eyes closed.

She opened her eyes and looked at him, her gaze taking several moments to focus on him. "No, it's fine. I'm starving."

"But I can get you whatever you want, and you can eat at the MacDonald's."

"I want to eat with you." She straightened and ran her fingers through her hair. "I'm ready. Let's go."

"All right." He got out of the rental car he'd picked up the day before. Tanner had driven his truck and towed the trailer down with their horses. Ethan wanted his own car so he could "explore San Antonio," which was code for "spend time alone with Brynn."

He didn't know if Tanner had deciphered the code or not, and he didn't much care. He didn't want to be tied to Tanner's truck and Tanner's schedule. At least they'd drawn back-to-back brackets, so he could watch her race, and she could see him rope. If he and Tanner made it to the semi-finals, they'd be in town for another eight days. He definitely wanted his freedom then.

She'd taken two steps toward the steakhouse when she stopped. "You know what? You're right. I don't want to eat out tonight." She curled herself into his body and held herself up by hanging onto his shoulders. "I am hungry. And I want to eat with you." She gazed up at him with adoration on her face.

Ethan didn't feel worthy of such a look, and he shifted his feet. "Want me to go order us something to go? We can eat in the car. Find a picnic table. Whatever you want."

She closed her eyes, and the moonlight on her face enhanced her beauty. He held her close, waiting for her response. When she didn't answer, he touched his lips to hers, a mere skate of skin on skin.

"Brynn? What do you want to eat?"

"Steak and salad." She tucked her head against his chest and swayed to music only she could hear.

"Okay, so are you gonna wait in the car?" Not that he wanted to let her go, but he was just as hungry as she claimed to be.

"Yeah." She flashed him a smile and returned to the passenger seat. Ethan watched her, a snag of worry arching through his mind. Was she okay? Should he take her home? Or did she always drift into a dreamlike state after a race?

He wasn't sure, as he'd never seen her perform before. After ordering and paying and waiting, he finally returned to the car with steak and salad for them both.

"No mashed potatoes?" she asked.

"Trying to be healthy for tomorrow." Ethan poured his bleu cheese dressing on his salad.

"I don't know how you eat that stuff." Brynn wrinkled her nose at the dressing.

"Like this." He stabbed a forkful of lettuce and olives and put it in his mouth. "Mmm. Its good."

She shook her head, though a smile played with her lips. "Ranch is so much better."

"Ranch is *bor*ing, cowgirl."

"Are you callin' me boring?" She looked at him like he'd just told her she hadn't qualified for the semis.

He shrugged and put another bite of salad in his mouth.

"Ethan," she warned.

He couldn't tell if she was flirting with him or being serious. He erred on the side of caution. "Brynn, all I know is that my life has gotten infinitely more interesting since you showed up."

Her boxy shoulders softened and she looked up through her lashes at him. She giggled and he chuckled and they finished their meal in comfortable silence.

THE NEXT MORNING, ETHAN'S NERVES FELT LIKE THEY'D BEEN electrocuted. He paced in the hotel room he and Tanner shared, the other man still snoring softly. After ten minutes, he left the room and headed over to the MacDonald's farm, where Tanner had boarded their horses.

Ethan didn't want to disturb anyone, and no one seemed to be outside. So he went in the barn and collected his rope. He'd thrown it two dozen times—each one hooking around the horns, thank you very much—before his phone rang.

"Where you at?" Tanner asked.

"Practicing," Ethan said. "Couldn't sleep."

"I'll be over in a half hour." Tanner hung up before Ethan could ask him to bring breakfast. He texted the request and went back to roping. He needed to work with Tiger, shave microseconds off his dally time, burst from the box with more speed.

But even after Tanner showed up with a bag of bagels, they didn't use their own horses. Tanner claimed he didn't want to tire them, that they'd only practice with them a few times before heading to the rodeo that evening.

Ethan nodded and agreed with whatever he said. Tanner had been here before; Ethan had not. The first time he participated in the rodeo, he'd only done bull riding. Roping was new to him, and team roping an entirely different language.

The day wore on. They practiced with their own horses—and Tiger's strength and size helped Ethan get the steer turned so much quicker than his practice horse.

They loaded up and headed to the rodeo grounds. Ethan changed into his official PRCA gear, put his competition number on his back, mounted Tiger, and lined up in the chute. He heard his name get called, and a beat of stunned silence. Or maybe he was imagining that part.

Then the announcer started saying something about his

previous career in rodeo, and the crowd erupted. He blocked them out the way he'd been training to do. He felt Tiger's muscles beneath him, focused on the steer in the chute to his right. He lifted his chin; the steer got released; he pounced.

His rope whipped around his head; his muscles knew exactly when to move and how far and with the right tension. The steer had taken two long strides, and he'd circled the rope twice, when he threw it. It landed perfectly, and he dallied and pulled left, hard, to get the steer's back legs in Tanner's reach.

Ethan hadn't breathed yet when Tanner had the heel loop under and the steer stretched between the two cowboys. He grinned and they followed the steer toward the other end of the arena.

Ethan wished he was as strong as Brynn and didn't need to know his time. But he glanced over his shoulder, and the red numbers on the scoreboard seared his retinas.

4.9.

He rode through the exit gate at the end of the arena, sure that time hadn't been right. But Tanner's whoop indicated that it was. A slow grin spread across his face.

"Four-point-nine seconds," he said to himself. They had to qualify for the semis with that. He put Tiger away, and by the time he finished, he knew he and Tanner had not only qualified for the semis, but won their bracket.

Now he had eight more days to practice—and spend time with Brynn. He couldn't stop smiling, no matter how hard he tried.

12

Brynn had never sat in the stands and watched a rodeo event before. She came, performed, escaped. But Ethan loved to sit and watch, and since they were both competing the following evening, she had nothing better to do but obsess over her horse and hang out with Daddy. Of the two, she preferred Ethan.

He made notes of who advanced in the team roping, but Brynn escaped to the concession stand and then the bathroom when the barrel racing started. She'd tucked her headphones and iPod in her purse, and she succeeded in drowning out the announcers until the event ended.

She wasn't sure why she didn't want to know. She'd kept track of times and who advanced at rodeos before. For some reason, though, she wanted to race cold in tomorrow's semi-finals.

She and Ethan had visited the Alamo earlier that day. They'd walked along the river, held hands, gone to lunches and dinners. Everything about San Antonio had been something from a movie, picture-perfect and serene.

Now you just need to win, she told herself as the rodeo ended and people began filing out of the stands. Ethan kept her close as they maneuvered through the crowd to his car. He drove her to the MacDonald's, where he asked, "You want to walk for a few minutes?"

The first time he'd asked, she hadn't understood the code. She did now. She grinned as she tucked her hand into his. "Sure thing."

He squeezed her fingers and they started their lazy walk around the perimeter of the property. In the back stood a hay barn, and Ethan had deemed it the perfect place to kiss her away from prying eyes.

Her heart thumped the closer they approached the barn. Even after a month with him, she still felt giddy with anticipation.

Sure enough, they'd barely rounded the corner when he pressed her into the wooden wall, swept his hat off, and pressed his lips to hers. These stolen kisses under the starlight made Brynn's heart race at the same time peace infused her soul. With a start, she realized she was falling in love with Ethan.

She deepened their kiss this time, wanting him to know without having to tell him. He must've sensed something, because he pulled back and brushed his fingers through her hair. "You're beautiful."

Brynn shivered, though the Texas night wasn't cold. "You're not so bad yourself."

He chuckled. "I should get you back to the house."

She slipped her fingers through his beltloops and kept him close. "You don't need to."

One of his eyebrows rose. "I don't?"

She leaned into him, tilted her head back, and waited for him to kiss her. As soon as he did, she murmured, "Not yet," and kissed him again with all the feelings she could muster.

BRYNN WOULDN'T ALLOW HERSELF TO SQUIRM IN HER SADDLE. Twenty barrel racers would compete tonight, and she'd drawn the thirteenth position. Alyssa had drawn twelfth.

Brynn kept her headphones in, and her music loud. She closed her eyes and shut out the bright rodeo lights, the darkening sky beyond the arena, the sight of the other cowgirls and their horses and racing sponsors.

Ethan, Chuck, and Daddy sat in the stands. She narrowed the crowd to only them, and with only three sets of eyes watching, her anxiety ebbed into the atmosphere around her.

Ethan had already performed, and he and Tanner had completed a clean run with a time of four-point-eight seconds. Good enough to advance to the finals. Brynn's lips buzzed with the kiss she'd given Ethan—in public, no less—as the names shone on the scoreboard.

Washington stood as still as a statue next to the fence, despite the chaos surrounding him. Brynn stole from the horse's strength, his calm demeanor.

Alyssa's horse shifted forward and back as she waited for the signal from the judge to go. She trotted him forward; the judge said go; the horse took off. Brynn closed her eyes. When the thundering of horse's hooves came back, she opened her eyes in time to see Alyssa turn the horse right, slow him, and exit the arena. She looked back, a huge smile on her face, and Brynn turned away and removed her earphones, tucking them in her shirt pocket.

Her turn. She moved Washington forward, feeling the tension in his muscles. "Okay, boy," she whispered to him. "Clean run. Right is no problem." She patted his neck and mentally went through the run one last time.

She ran him, got the signal, and spurred him forward with everything she had. He took the first barrel flawlessly, the second without problem. She spurred him toward three, her legs flapping against his sides as he streaked down the arena.

Step, turn, step, turn, and she clenched her teeth as she urged the horse back to where they'd started. The announcer screamed her time over the speaker system, but it blurred in her ears as she directed Washington out of the arena.

With only six riders after her, she'd have to hustle to get Washington cared for before the award announcements. The staff member came around, gathering the riders, and Brynn had to line up next to Alyssa as they made their way out. Her boots squished in the dirt. Uncertainty spread through her like a disease.

Her name sat at the top of the earnings board after the bracket round. The number wasn't worth writing home about, but after tonight, if she'd done well enough, she should be close to ten grand—and a spot in the finals, where she could make up to fifteen thousand more.

She kept her eyes forward, her smile hitched in place. The announcer said, "Put your hands together for the ladies of the PRWA!" The crowd obliged, and the names and times flashed on the screen.

Hers sat in second place, with a time of thirteen-point-nine-nine. Above her was *Alyssa Shumway, 13.92.*

She turned to Alyssa and extended her hand. "Congratulations."

Alyssa knew how to play to the crowd and the press too. She shook Brynn's hand and smiled. That screen faded and listed the top five money winners that would be advancing from this semi-final into the finals.

Brynn was second there too. Alyssa was first.

Doesn't matter, she told herself as the twenty women filed out of the arena. *You made it. She's only five hundred dollars ahead of you.*

But if Alyssa won the finals too, she'd still be in first.

She won't win the finals, Brynn told herself as Ethan scooped her into a bear hug with a scowling Alyssa right behind him.

IN THE FINALS, THE TEAM ROPING EVENT FOLLOWED THE BARREL racing, so Ethan couldn't sit in the stands and watch Brynn. He'd given Chuck explicit instructions to text her time and the final placings as soon as he knew them, so he could run out and watch her accept her money—and a medal, if she won.

They'd drawn to go last in the roping, so he'd have time to see her for a few minutes before Tanner would expect him to be back.

His phone went off as he threw a practice loop toward a dummy. He flinched, and missed. Tanner frowned. Ethan checked his phone, unconcerned about Tanner. In every practice run, Ethan and Tiger gave Tanner the perfect steer to rope. Together, they'd been flawless in Texas.

Chuck had texted. *13.79.*

Ethan's grin exploded onto his face. She had to win with that. A vein of sourness coasted through his stomach. He didn't want Brynn to lose to Alyssa, who he'd learned was her biggest rival. There was something more between the two women, but Ethan didn't need to know what it was to want Brynn to beat Alyssa.

Two riders left.

Ethan stuck his phone in his pocket and abandoned his rope on a nearby peg. "I'm gonna go see who wins barrel racing."

Tanner growled, but Ethan strode past him. "Relax, Tanner. Our performance is at least a half hour away."

"I need you ready," he called after Ethan.

"I'm ready now," he yelled back.

He arrived in the stands just as the tail of the last rider disappeared under the stands. "Hey," he said to Chuck. "What were the other times?"

Chuck grinned. "She won. Alyssa knocked over a barrel."

Fireworks popped in Ethan's chest. His fist curled and he knocked it against Chuck's. "Yes."

Minutes later, the cowgirls came out, with Brynn's name shining at the top of the winner's list. The announcer went through each one, and when he said, "And your San Antonio champion, and big money winner, with a total of twenty-five thousand, seven hundred and thirty-four dollars...Brynn Bowman!"

Ethan cheered with the rest of the crowd, clapped Chuck on the shoulder, nodded to Brynn's father, and headed out. He wanted to be in the tunnel to meet Brynn.

Instead, he met Tanner's angry glare. "C'mon," he said, already heading back to the waiting area where all the teams threw ropes and fussed with their horses.

"I want to see Brynn first."

"They'll be ten minutes takin' pictures."

"Which means we have time before our event."

"Let's throw a few before she comes out."

Reluctantly, Ethan followed him. He tossed a couple of times, each one hitting their mark though his mind lingered on a certain dark-haired cowgirl. It had been a long time since Ethan had been so preoccupied with a woman. A long time since he'd felt the things now running through him. He liked more than the way she looked. He liked her strong spirit, her iron will, her caring and generous side. He liked the vulnerability he'd seen in her, the way she let down her walls around him.

He threw again, and missed. Tanner glared.

"What?" Ethan asked. "It's the first one I've missed all night."

"I don't like it."

"Like what?"

He waved back toward the arena. "You and Brynn."

His words landed like a sucker punch. "Because *you* still like her."

Tanner chuckled darkly. "Please. That's not why. She's a distraction."

"She is not. She won't even be at half the rodeos we go to. It's not a problem."

Tanner moved closer, his dark eyes storming. "You serious about her?"

Ethan glared and gave Tanner's attitude right back to him. "Why do you care?"

"I care about her. She's my friend."

"And she does massive favors for you." Ethan still hadn't asked Brynn why she'd been the one to drive down to Three Rivers and recruit him to be Tanner's header. "And keeps keys for you. You sure you're not jealous?"

"I just want to know what she is to you. She doesn't deserve to be hurt."

"I like her," Ethan said. "She's a great horseback rider." He wasn't about to tell Tanner about the hand-holding, the secret rendezvous behind the barn. Tanner didn't need to know that Ethan fell asleep every night with Brynn's face in his mind and the vanilla taste of her lips in his mouth.

"A great horseback rider?"

"One of the best I've seen," Ethan said. "I like watching her compete. It's incredible."

The team roping event got called, and a flurry of activity stopped their conversation. Tanner's eyes burned into Ethan. "Let's do this."

"Never been more ready," he said. He glanced toward the path that led from the arena, seeing a couple of barrel racers. He scanned the area, his heart palpitating with fear that he'd missed Brynn.

He didn't see her. He waited another few seconds. A few more. The teams started to move out of the holding area. Disappointed, he went to mount Tiger. After all, Ethan had a team roping competition to win.

13

B rynn made it to the bathroom and behind a locked door before she allowed Ethan's words to repeat themselves.

I like her. She's a great horseback rider.

It wasn't the worst thing he could've said. But it wasn't what she wanted him to say when someone asked him about her. She wasn't sure why Tanner had even asked—she'd overheard them talking in the middle of their conversation. Tanner had said, "I want to know what she is to you." The part about him not wanting her to get hurt was actually kind of nice of him. Tanner normally didn't care about anyone but himself.

She'd been surprised at the way she wanted Ethan to react. The word *girlfriend* had popped into her mind. She wanted him to tell Tanner she was his girlfriend. When he hadn't—when he'd said she was a good horseback rider, she'd fled.

You're more than that to him, she told herself. *You always have been.*

She wiped her face though she hadn't cried and exited the stall. She'd just won the barrel racing event in one of the largest regular season rodeos. She'd need to be on, look perfect, until she made it back to the MacDonald's house and could shower away this day.

She returned to the room where she'd left her stuff and quickly changed. Ethan was more than a great horseback rider to her, and despite the river of pain flowing through her core, she wanted to watch him rope.

Brynn settled next to Chuck with three teams still to go before Tanner and Ethan.

"Great job!" Chuck engulfed her in a hug, and Daddy passed her a wide grin and a folder with all the times. She took it, only because it would have her check inside. Daddy would've gone down to the booth where all the participants checked in and out and taken care of everything. He always did.

She leaned over Chuck. "Thanks, Daddy." Through the roar of the crowd, she wasn't sure if the level of gratitude she'd tried to infuse into her voice had reached his ears.

He patted her hand with his weathered one, and Brynn wondered how she could take the rodeo from him. If she quit, he would have no reason to keep track of times, arrange travel, shop for the best barrel racing horses.

She sat up straight, avoiding Chuck's eye. He nudged her with his elbow, but she shook her head. The only thing that saved her from Chuck's relentless nature was the roar of the crowd as a team of ropers scored a four-point-three on their flawless run.

Ethan wouldn't be able to beat that. Brynn squared her shoulders, the hope she held for his success refusing to drain.

"You okay?" her brother asked.

"Fine."

"You look a little flushed."

"It's hot in here. There're twenty thousand people crammed in this arena."

"Why'd you thank Daddy?"

She turned and glared at Chuck. "I always tell Daddy thank you."

"Not until later." He glanced at the folder. "You never carry that out. The only time you touch it is to sign the check that I then deposit."

The announcer came on and started talking about the next team. Brynn took a deep, deep breath and seized the opportunity. "I'm thinkin' of quitting the rodeo," she said, barely loud enough for Chuck to hear.

He'd been leaning down to hear, and he jerked back, his eyes wide. "You are?"

She shook her head as Daddy glanced over at them. Luckily, Chuck caught her drift, and he stopped asking questions. But he now wore a surprised, puzzled look. Brynn slumped on the bench seat. She shouldn't have told him. Should've kept her secret, the way she'd planned, until December.

She didn't think Chuck would tell Daddy, but he could tell Ethan, and Brynn didn't want him to know either.

"Don't tell anyone," she said as the crowd applauded for the cowboys as they rode out of the arena. "This is Ethan," she said louder, so Daddy could hear.

She clasped her hands together and brought them to her chin. She wanted him to win so badly. But four-point-three seconds. They couldn't beat that. Could they?

Across from her, Ethan jerked his head. The steer's cage opened, and it shot out, Ethan and Tanner in hot pursuit.

Ethan looked absolutely flawless on his broad chestnut horse. His rope flew, hit its mark, and he yanked the horse left. Tanner had the back legs tied before she could breathe, and her eyes flew to the clock.

4.5.

Since she didn't pay attention to the numbers, she didn't know what their earnings were coming into the finals. Ethan had been more than kind, keeping such things to himself. In fact, they spoke little about the rodeo. Brynn realized that he'd done that for her, and rush of gratitude and—dare she admit it?—love hit her square in the chest.

She flipped open the folder as the announcer said, "And that'll do it for this year's team roping. Go ahead and clap for our last team as they head on out."

She flipped pages until sure enough, she found the one Daddy had written the team roping rankings on. She scanned, trying to find the names and numbers before the announcer said anything. She found them—Tanner/Ethan—in second place coming into the finals.

They'd probably stay there.

"And we have your winners!" The announcer paused as the names and earnings flashed on the big screen.

Sure enough, Tanner Wolf and Ethan Greene sat in second position, with earnings of just over seventeen thousand dollars. Each.

She stood and whistled and clapped as loud as she could when their names were announced and they came out of the underground tunnel in front of her. "Ethan!" she called.

He turned, found her frantically waving her arms, and grinned in her direction. He blew her a kiss, and turned around to lean against the fence. Tanner stepped close to him, saying something, and Ethan shook his head.

She watched Tanner accept the plaque, and then she focused on Ethan. He couldn't seem to stop smiling as he too watched Tanner.

When the awards ended, she hurried out of the stands and toward the stables. Surely Tanner and Ethan hadn't had time to take care of the horses. She arrived before they did, and when Ethan rounded the corner and saw her there, she hurtled herself at him.

He caught her around the waist as he laughed. Happiness, stronger than she'd ever known, flowed through her.

Brynn found her feet and pressed her lips to Ethan's. "Second place!" She beamed at him. "That's amazing, you know. First time being head horse and getting second place?" She stepped out of his arms to congratulate Tanner, who wore a look on his face halfway between amusement and anger.

When she stepped back to Ethan, most of the excitement near the stables had died down. She raised herself up so her mouth was level with his ear. He leaned toward her, one arm securely slung around her waist. "I think you're a really great horseback rider."

He stumbled-stepped away from her, pure panic parading across his face.

She cocked one eyebrow, spun on her booted heel, and walked away. "Meet you at the car," she called over her shoulder.

ETHAN FUMED, MOSTLY AT TANNER. A LITTLE BIT AT HIMSELF FOR saying he thought Brynn was a great horseback rider. She'd obviously overheard him—and didn't seem too happy about such a comment.

He'd explain everything as soon as he could get out of the arena—but Tanner wanted to talk about their upcoming schedule before they left for the night. With the rodeo over, the scheduling did need to be done. But Tanner could text. Or wait until they got back to the hotel room they shared.

Ethan shoved away his restlessness and impatience with Tanner. The cowboy had allowed him to join his already sponsored team. He'd fixed him up with a horse to ride. He'd taken care of all the rodeo fees, the travel expenses, everything. All Ethan focused on was practicing and showing up. He could give Tanner fifteen minutes.

"So we'll be headin' to Arcadia—that's in Florida—next weekend," Tanner said. "Smaller rodeo. Two nights, with a qualifying round on Thursday before brackets on Friday." He handed Ethan a manila folder stuffed with papers. "Then we'll be in Georgia, and then Montgomery. It's a decent-sized rodeo. Three full nights. Then we'll be back in Texas, in Austin, for another leg of the Million Dollar Tour."

Ethan nodded through it all, promised to be in Florida by Tuesday, and to keep practicing in between, and thanked Tanner for everything.

By the time he made it to the car, most of the other vehicles in the lot had cleared out. He stumbled when he saw Brynn sittin' on the hood, the moon shining on her cowgirl hat and illuminating the silver on the toes of her boots.

She glanced up at his approach, barely lifting her head enough for her to see under the brim of her hat.

"Tanner has us in a new city every week in March." Ethan unlocked the car and dumped the folders in the backseat before joining her by leaning against the hood of the car.

"He tends to do that," she said. "I think he did ninety rodeos last year."

He grunted, his dedication to staying through the year waning. He contemplated the stars for a few seconds, trying to gather his thoughts. "So you won."

"Yeah."

Ethan turned toward her, tired of the games. "You *are* the best horseback rider I've ever watched."

Her eyes flashed with anger, but he forged on. "And whenever I see you, my breath catches. Every time." He slid his hand around the back of her neck, slipped down the length of her braid, where he took out the elastic holding it in place and combed his fingers through her hair. "When I think about you, I can't sleep."

"But you told Tanner you 'liked me' and—"

"I know what I told Tanner." He let out a frustrated sigh. "Did you consider that maybe I don't want Tanner to know the depth of my feelin's for you? That maybe I'm not the kind of cowboy that kisses and tells?"

"But you *are* a cowboy."

He frowned. "That's never been a secret." Cocking his head to the side, he tried to get a read on her. "Why don't you like cowboys? Is it because you and Tanner—?" He cut off, not quite sure what "she and Tanner" had been to each other.

"Did he tell you about us?"

"Not really. Mentioned you guys had tried being together." Ethan shrugged like he didn't care, but curiosity burned a blazing path through him.

"He's only one reason. Every other guy I've dated are the others."

"Are there a lot of others?" He couldn't keep the interest—and the jealousy—from infusing his words.

She smiled. "A few. Not a lot." Brynn looked away, her jaw jumping. Ethan had seen this strategy before—she ground her teeth whenever she needed to work up to saying something hard. "A fiancé."

Ethan let the word, and the meaning of it, roll around in his head. He didn't mind that Brynn had a past, maybe one she wasn't proud of. If he understood one thing, it was that.

Help me, he prayed. *What do I say here?*

"He still around?" Ethan asked, his fingers trailing up her arm to her shoulder and back to her wrist.

"No. He retired from the rodeo right after he ran off with Alyssa." She met his gaze, fire and ice in her eyes at the same time.

Ethan's chest collapsed on itself, and he couldn't get a decent breath. He leaned down and kissed her, a quick peck on the mouth. "I'm so sorry." He wrapped her in his arms and held tight. She didn't cry; Ethan supposed she'd moved past that.

"That's why I drove down to Texas to recruit you to be Tanner's header," she said into his chest. "He wanted to ask my ex-fiancé to join up again. We fought about it for a long time, until finally he said I needed to get you on-board so he wouldn't have to ask Dave."

Something caught in Ethan's chest. Brynn hadn't done a favor for Tanner when she'd driven to Three Rivers. She'd been taking care of herself. "Ah, so there's the *Da*."

She sighed into him, a small laugh bubbling against his chest. "Yep. There he is."

The people and events in the rodeo had always been a twisted, tangled mess. And Brynn had been doing it for years. He wanted to protect her from that labyrinth. "So when Tanner came to get keys from you...?"

She pulled back a bit. "Keys from me?" She shook her head. "I never had any keys of his."

"Yeah," Ethan said. "Remember, it was one of my first nights in town. I said I was with Tanner when he stopped by your place."

"Duke boards his horses. Tanner got the keys from him." She searched Ethan's face. "You been worried about something still hanging on between me and Tanner?"

"He likes pretty women," Ethan said by way of explanation, wishing the vein of foolishness hadn't exploded through him quite so fast. But when she spoke such sentences like they were made of complete garbage, embarrassment did coat his throat. "And I saw him kiss you in the hall at the training facility that first day."

"What on earth...?" The wheels started turning in her head, if her astounded look was any indiacation.

"Tanner said you had keys of his he needed," Ethan continued. "Not Duke."

"He's a liar," Brynn said, her tone darkening with the color of her eyes. "Probably wanted you to think I was taken. He doesn't like having a girlfriend during the circuit, which is all the time. That's why we didn't work out. The man is married to the rodeo."

Ethan's insides softened. "He mentioned he didn't like me being with you. Said I was distracted."

"Sounds like him." She glanced back toward the arena. "I remember that first day. He did kiss me on the cheek in the hall. He was...nice that day. It was strange. He said he hoped he hadn't hurt me, and that I deserved someone great. Said he was real sorry it hadn't worked out for us." She brought her hand to her cheek again, as if the brand of Tanner's lips still lingered there. "It was weird."

Ethan couldn't help the chuckle that came from his mouth. "That kiss unsettled me somethin' fierce. It's why I went to dinner with Alyssa that night, and why I didn't call you for two weeks. Why I couldn't go to church with you when you asked." He dipped his head and touched his lips to her cheek—to the same spot Tanner had kissed.

Brynn seemed to melt into Ethan's touch, and he liked the rush that roared through him.

"So." She bumped his chest with her shoulder. "Say you had a friend that you could tell about me. What would you tell them if they asked what Tanner did?"

His lungs squeezed. "What did Tanner ask again?"

She nudged his ribs with her elbow, barely a touch at all. "He asked what I am to you."

"And this is someone I trust askin'?" Ethan's mind circled and swirled. "Someone I can be honest with? Someone who won't judge me?"

"Yes." The night almost swallowed her voice before he heard it.

Ethan figured he might as well lay all his cards on the table. "I'd tell them you were my girlfriend. If they asked to do something with me, but I could do something with you instead, I'd choose you." He exhaled and inhaled the scent of Brynn, a mixture of horse and dirt and flowers.

She snuggled into his side, and he sent a prayer of gratitude to the Lord that he'd been able to find and vocalize the right words.

"I'd choose you too," she said, and the words sank right into the fleshy parts of Ethan's cowboy heart. He had no idea being with a woman could be so perfect. He closed his eyes and pulled Brynn closer.

14

B rynn traveled to Lousianna and then back to Texas for rodeos. She texted Ethan late at night, after Chuck and Daddy snored in their beds, after she'd spent hours in the saddle, or evenings with her headphones blocking out all distractions.

He always texted back immediately, like he was lying awake, waiting for her to message. Of course, he initiated the conversation sometimes too, but he usually texted during the day, something funny about what his trainer made him eat, or a silly story about something that had happened with one of the horses, or how exciting it was to be back in the bull riding circuit again.

She wished she'd been able to see him tame a bull in San Antonio, but he'd been too new to put on the docket. Though he'd been a champion before, he hadn't been on a bull in six years, and he couldn't enter in that event at such a big rodeo.

As the date of the next pro rodeo in Austin drew near, Brynn anticipated seeing Ethan again for the first time in almost three weeks. A hole existed in her life, wider and deeper than she thought possible, without him to see and touch and kiss everyday.

Every event she performed in, she felt closer and closer to quitting. Chuck finally cornered her one night by knocking on her hotel room door and then using the key she'd given him to enter.

"C'mon in." She glanced up from her laptop, where she was studying the tape of her latest run in Scottsdale.

"Sorry to barge in."

She leaned back in the desk chair. "You are not." Brynn added a smile to the statement so Chuck would know she wasn't really upset.

"I've been thinkin' about what you said." He sat on the edge of the bed to her right.

Brynn's eyebrows drew together. "What did I say?"

"Couple of weeks ago? About quittin' the rodeo?"

Cold fear danced across her skin. "I don't want to talk about it, Chuck." She turned back to her laptop.

"Daddy's ready too," Chuck said.

Brynn deliberately kept her attention on the screen, though she wasn't seeing anything. "What does that mean?"

"Haven't you noticed how tired he is?" Chuck asked. "He hasn't stopped coughing since San Antonio. It's not bad—just an annoyance—but he's still not well."

Brynn *had* noticed Daddy moving slower when he loaded and unloaded Washington, fighting off a lingering cough, and sleeping later each day. She hadn't known what to say. If she asked, he'd just tell her he was fine and continue about his work. It would take two broken legs to keep Daddy down, and maybe not even then.

"He's doing this for you." Chuck folded his arms. "Which would be fine—if it's what you wanted. But—"

"It *is* what I want." Brynn speared him with a heated look. "He wants me to be the World Champion. I'm going to do that for him."

Chuck set his mouth in a firm line. "And then you're going to quit."

"That's the plan." The words tasted like ash in Brynn's mouth. She couldn't tell Chuck how much she wanted to quit right now. Even if Daddy was moving slower, she knew he'd be disappointed if she quit without at least trying to win the World.

An image of Three Rivers Ranch floated through her frenzied mind, infusing that sense of peace she'd felt in the short time she was there. Maybe she could return to that beautiful country— especially if Ethan....

She let the idea linger, but the image of the perfect, peaceful existence got shattered by Chuck's voice saying, "Well, your plan isn't working that great, Brynn. Have you noticed you're fifth on the money boards?" He got up and walked out before she could reply. Of course she knew where she stood.

She just couldn't muster up the energy to care.

Brynn frowned at her computer screen, the image of Daddy's tired, lined face in her mind's eye. "Maybe I *should* just quit now."

Brynn escaped the stuffiness of her hotel room, with all the words Chuck had spoken trapped in the air, by calling a cab and paying him to wait while she visited the barn. Washington seemed content, happy, and eagerly came over as she wandered the aisles in the boarding stables. Just stroking her fingers along Washington's neck infused her with the peace she'd been missing.

Her phone sang her country ringtone, indicating she'd gotten a text. She didn't check it, though it was probably Ethan. She wasn't sure why she didn't swipe open the text immediately. Probably because she didn't want to read about how awesome the rodeo was.

Not fair, she thought. Ethan deserved to be happy, and if he enjoyed bull riding, she should be glad he'd found something to like when he thought he wouldn't.

She sighed, and Washington's ear flickered.

Her mind ran rampant with Ethan in the rodeo, and she imagined him finding some flaxen-haired beauty on one of his tour stops. They'd hit it off, and laugh the night away, and he'd text less and less. Eventually, he'd break up with her, the way all the other cowboys had.

Something tight pulled in her middle, and she couldn't get a proper breath. What had she been thinking, starting a relationship with Ethan? It obviously couldn't work.

Trying to push the poisonous thoughts away, Brynn pulled her phone from her pocket and checked it. Ethan hadn't texted, but Chuck. *Where'd you go?*

Of course Ethan hadn't texted. He was too busy with whoever he'd met in Montgomery. *Stop it*, she told herself. She tapped out a message to Chuck, telling him she'd gone to visit Washington. To make her mind stop conjuring things that weren't true, she texted Ethan too.

What's going on today?

He didn't answer immediately, which only darkened her mood. She put her feet to walking, the way she did when she felt this caged, this trapped, inside her own life. She'd started thinking of her walks around her Texas neighborhood as her escape route. Escape from her mother's death. Escape from moving to a new state.

Escape from the rodeo.

The more she thought about cosmetology school, the more she didn't want to do it.

So what do you want?

She wasn't sure, and as she walked, she turned her thoughts toward heaven. She'd never asked the Lord what *He* wanted her to do, how *He* could help her, but as night fell, she did.

The sky didn't split open. Thoughts barely filtered through

her mind. Behind her, the soft whinny of a horse broke the starry silence.

Horses.

Should she do something with horses? Brynn turned and wandered back through the barn. She already had a career with horses. More confused than ever, Brynn returned to the cab and asked him to drive her back to the hotel.

———

ETHAN FELL INTO BED, HIS MIND NUMB WITH HAPPINESS. HE'D JUST won the bull riding event at the Montgomery rodeo.

Beaten Tanner by point-one of a point.

Beaten everyone.

The perma-smile he'd been wearing for an hour pulled against his cheeks, and he bolted to a sitting position and fumbled for his phone to dial Brynn. She'd texted earlier—during his practice rounds—but now she didn't answer. He held his cell away from his ear to check the time. Not even ten yet. She should be awake.

His disappointment lasted only a moment, barely dinging against the surface of his joy. He remembered the thrill of winning, of being on the bull as it did everything in its power to buck, and twist, and throw him off.

Tonight, he'd conquered it for the first time in a long time. He hadn't been as successful in Florida, at either of the rodeos where he and Tanner had performed. But tonight....

Ethan relived the scent of the dirt, the mass of the bull he'd drawn, Plays For Keeps, beneath him. He'd wrapped the rope so tight, so tight, pinning his hand to the animal.

The buzzer sounded.

The gate opened.

The bull bolted.

Everything narrowed to just him and the counterweight of his arm, anticipating the direction the bull would flip next. When the bell had sounded signaling his eight second ride, Ethan had started smiling.

He hadn't stopped since.

Tanner had achieved an eight second ride too, but the cowboys who accomplished that were then judged. And Ethan's ride had been judged as superior.

He exhaled as his stomach roared. Tanner always went out after the rodeo; Ethan usually ordered room service or had his friend stop by a drive-through before getting dropped off at the hotel.

Ethan liked his time alone. It reminded him of ranching, of being on the wide open range by himself, with only the wind, and the pure blue sky, and God. Brynn had filled his down hours, and he glanced at his phone again.

She'd return his call when she saw it. He swung his legs off the bed and stood, patting his back pocket to make sure he had his wallet with him. A stop at the front desk provided him with the name of the best restaurant for steak and seafood, as well as a way to get there. The cab the concierge had called rolled into the circle drive only ten minutes later, and Ethan went out to celebrate.

Turned out, celebrating alone wasn't all that fun. He didn't drink, and he didn't sing karaoke, and he didn't like sitting in the booth by himself when everyone else seemed to have someone to celebrate with. But the steak and shrimp tasted like nothing he'd ever had before, even in Texas. Even at Three Rivers Ranch.

His heart jumped at the thought of the ranch he loved. The ranch he'd left only a few months ago. His plan had always been to go back, and go back as soon as possible. But winning events provided a rush he'd never felt while hauling hay or branding calves or repairing tractors.

While eating, he also remembered why he'd left the rodeo circuit in the first place. But he wasn't the same man who was looking for love in all the wrong places, and partying like every bull ride made him into a superhero.

He was older now. Wiser. Attached.

His phone rang as if his thoughts had summoned Brynn to call. He gulped a mouthful of water and picked up the call. "Brynn!" he practically yelled to be heard above the country music a redheaded woman had just cued up on the karaoke stage.

"Ethan? Where are you?"

He glanced around. "Not sure. This place the concierge at the hotel recommended. Best steak and seafood in town, and he was right."

"Having—" She cut out, and Ethan adjusted the phone against his ear.

"Sorry, Brynn. You cut out. I didn't hear what you said." The waitress approached and gestured to his water. He shook his head, and she moved on.

"I asked if you were having fun." Her words carried a bite of acidity.

"Not really," he said. "It'd be better if you were here. But listen, I have great news. I won the bull riding event in Montgomery!"

She said something that sounded congratulatory, but Ethan still couldn't quite understand her. So he talked, hoping she could hear him. He told her about drawing the toughest bull, with the highest throw ratio, and said that was probably why he'd won.

He didn't care. He'd won, and he didn't care much how.

When he finally finished, Brynn said, "That's great, Ethan," and her voice sounded tinny and quiet.

"Can't wait for Austin," he said. "Just a few more days."

"Just a few more days," she echoed, and their call ended.

Ethan finished eating as quickly as possible after that, pulling his hat lower when a group of cowgirls came in, twittering and sweeping the restaurant for potential dates. He wasn't interested, but as he stood to leave, one of the women draped herself over his arm.

"Hey, didn't you win the bull ride tonight?"

He nodded and extracted his arm from beneath both her hands. "Ma'am."

She giggled, leaned closer to him like she'd kiss him right here, right now, and put both hands on his shoulders. "What's your name?"

"Uh." He tried to back up, but he met the wall. He couldn't push her away—what if she fell? He cast a look around the restaurant, and his waitress caught his eye. She gestured toward someone Ethan couldn't see, and a man wearing all black came over.

Ethan escaped while the two talked, while the woman rejoined her friends, a definite pout on her lips.

"Thanks," he said to the waitress as he passed.

"Never had to help a man get out of a sticky situation," she said. "Especially one as handsome as you."

Ethan flashed her a tight smile and exited into the night. He'd definitely be sticking to room service from now on.

15

Brynn slept poorly leading up to the rodeo in Austin. After Ethan's phone call—which sounded like he'd been in a karaoke bar—her heart felt three sizes too small. With her only answer of horses as what she should do with her life, she'd taken to spending longer hours with Washington.

She didn't always work him through the triangular pattern of the barrels, but simply rode him around the farm where he'd been boarded for the past week. The easy, gentle clomp-clomp of his hooves soothed her, but she found the most joy when training with him.

She prepared for the qualifying run on Thursday by plugging in her headphones and disappearing behind Daddy's presence. He took care of everything, and Brynn couldn't get her horse where he needed to be—let alone herself—without him.

"Thanks, Daddy." She gripped him in a tight hug he returned.

He didn't let her go as quickly as he usually did. "You okay, baby?"

Emotion crowded her throat; the words she'd been collecting gathered in her mouth. She cleared them away. "I'm fine."

"You don't seem to be havin' fun this year." He pulled back and fixed his wizened gaze on her.

Her heart tried to vault out of her chest. He knew she wanted to quit. Had Chuck told him? Let something suggestive slip?

She took a deep breath, the confession there, ready to come out. But one look at his open, honest face, and she couldn't tell him. "I'm doin' the best I can." That was the truth, in more ways than one.

He looked over her shoulder, off into the distance, to something inside his mind. "Your mama told me not to push you," he said, his attention coming back to Brynn. "So let me know if I'm pushin' you too hard."

Brynn didn't know what to say. Heat gathered behind her eyes, but she willed it to cool. She didn't want to cry before she performed. Hated crying in general. So she merely nodded.

He took a big breath and released it. "Competition is as fierce here as it was in San Antonio. We'll be in Indio next week, and it'll be easier there."

Brynn focused on her upcoming performance, the way she had countless times before. No emotions during a run. Just focus. She listened to her father remind her to spur harder during the final sprint, to keep that knee tucked on the second turn. She nodded along with him, though she'd heard it all before. Though she could train any horse to be a champion barrel racer.

Lightning struck her thoughts. She could train any horse to be a champion barrel racer. A beam of sunlight shone on her, as if from heaven, and she knew training barrel horses was what she wanted to do with her life.

With this newfound knowledge—and freedom—Brynn flew through her warm-ups and dominated the qualifying round. Ethan was mysteriously absent, though he should've arrived in Austin last night. This morning at the latest.

Not many people chose to watch the qualifying rounds in the hours before lunch—before the main events of the evening—but he'd said he'd be there to see her. Even asked about going to lunch together afterward.

Brynn would ride in all three rounds, and if she won, she could top the earnings list come Saturday night. With the promise of a future with horses but without the rodeo, she smiled true for the first time in weeks.

———

TANNER CALLED JUST AFTER LUNCH, WHICH BRYNN HAD EATEN WITH Chuck and Daddy. "Tanner?" she answered. "Where are you guys?"

"I just pulled into town. Ran into some trouble this morning with the trailer. You seen Ethan around the practice fields?"

"No." Brynn frowned and looked at Chuck. "Ethan's not here." Unease coated her voice, cut through her core. "He didn't ride with you?" Tanner liked his header in the truck with him so they could visualize together, talk, bond, whatever men did to get along.

"He said he was gonna catch a ride so he could get there early enough to see you."

Her heart grew one size. Maybe he hadn't found another cowgirl to entertain him. The fact that Brynn still believed he would only reminded her of her own unresolved issues.

Brynn stood like she'd see Ethan scanning the rodeo grounds for her. They'd gotten lunch at a deli and brought it back to the picnic tables at the adjacent park. "He's not here, Tanner."

"I'll call him. Don't go worryin' your pretty little head. I was just wondering how the place looks."

"Looks like there's gonna be three days of rodeo," Brynn said, surprised she was still able to employ her sarcasm when Ethan should be here, but wasn't. "Call me back as soon as you hear from him."

Like she couldn't call him herself. She dialed him, her anxiety growing like weeds with every ring.

"Hello?" a woman answered.

Brynn's blood turned to ice. She couldn't get her voice out of her mouth.

"Hello?" the woman asked again, more annoyance in her tone this time.

"I—I'm looking for Ethan Greene," Brynn managed.

"Cowboy, right?"

The woman didn't even know who he was? Brynn's defenses rose. "Yeah. He's a cowboy all right." Bitterness coated the words.

"Dropped him off Georgetown. Wasn't comin' all the way down to Austin."

"How long ago?" Brynn asked.

"'Bout ten minutes. He left his phone in my console."

"Thanks." Brynn hung up, unsure of what to do. Georgetown was only about thirty miles north of Austin. She could take Daddy's truck and go get Ethan. Be back in less than an hour. But she had no way of contacting him. No way of knowing where he was.

While she stood thinking, her phone rang. She glanced at it, barely registering the vibrations against her palm. She didn't know the number.

Hope flared in her chest. "Ethan?" she answered.

"Hey, cowgirl." He sounded casual and unafraid. Typical Ethan. Whatever life threw at him, he juggled and tamed it into submission.

"Where are you?" she asked. "Tanner just called and said you got a ride with someone else, and I tried callin' you, but some woman answered."

"Wonder if you might be able to come pick me up." He chuckled. "It's been quite the morning."

"Tell me where you are, and I'll be there as soon as I can." Her words may have come out a little strong, but she didn't care. She was already keeping things from Daddy, and she wanted everything in the open with someone. With Ethan.

ETHAN PACED THE SIDEWALK IN FRONT OF THE GAS STATION WHERE LuAnn had dropped him. She'd barely turned the corner when he realized he didn't have his phone with him. His duffle, yes. His wallet, sure. But not his phone. And he felt crippled without it.

It had taken him several minutes to find someone willing to let him borrow their phone, and now he just had to wait for Brynn to come.

He should enjoy the downtime, but his thoughts ran in circles around Brynn. The thought of returning to Three Rivers —or Colorado Springs, if he decided the siren's call of bull riding proved too loud—without her made a hole widen in his chest.

Things seemed to change on a daily basis, and Ethan wasn't sure what his plans were for the future, but he wanted her in it. He was no closer to a solution when she pulled up in her father's giant pickup truck.

She jumped out of the driver's seat and hurried around the hood to embrace him. He grinned as he wrapped his arms around her. He inhaled the floral scent of her hair, tucked his face in the softness of her neck, and couldn't wait another second to kiss her.

The first touch of her lips to his in over three weeks sent Ethan's adrenaline through the roof. He really wished he'd been able to make it to Austin this morning so he could have this reunion in a more private location.

Brynn obviously wanted the same thing, because she pulled away sooner than he liked. "You're okay."

"I'm fine." He trailed his fingers along her braid and kept her tucked against his body. "How was your run this morning?"

"Great." She beamed up into his face. "I'm first going into tonight."

He grinned down at her. "Of course you are."

"Should we get going? Tanner seemed about to have an aneurism when I told him you were in Georgetown and I was comin' to get you."

Ethan's smile faltered. "Tanner can wait." But he moved toward the truck anyway, sliding all the way across the bench seat so he could ride with his leg pressing against Brynn's as she drove.

She put the vehicle in drive and dropped her hand to curl around his, which rested on her knee. "I missed you," he murmured, leaning over to taste his favored spot just below her ear.

She giggled, sighed, and leaned into another kiss. "Behave yourself."

"I am," he said. "Did you miss me too?"

"Like crazy," she said, her matter-of-fact tone glazed with something more. Something deeper. Ethan sat up straight to behave himself, the familiar worry over the future returning in full force.

"Brynn?"

She didn't take her eyes from the road. "Yeah?"

"What if I wanted to stay in the rodeo circuit?"

She blinked rapidly, but otherwise showed no reaction. "You like bull riding." It wasn't a question.

"I like winning," he admitted.

"Winning isn't everything," she muttered.

"I know it isn't." Ethan knew better than most, actually. Knew that winning one thing sometimes meant losing another. His brain teemed, pulsed against his skull. Was he making the same mistake he had with Suzy? Couldn't he have a career *and* a family?

He wasn't sure, and he didn't know, and nothing lined up or

made sense. Ethan kept his eyes focused out the window, glad when Brynn mentioned her father and how he still hadn't quite recovered from his illness in San Antonio. The non-rodeo conversation allowed him to keep his thoughts to himself—and he didn't want to tell Brynn he might stay on the circuit. She'd be staying too, so maybe trying to boost his bull riding ranking was a good choice.

Ethan honestly didn't trust himself to make a decision about rodeo—or Brynn—right now. So he asked her about her father, and if she'd thought any more about cosmetology school.

She sighed. "Yeah, I don't think I'm going to do that."

"Change of heart? Different plan?"

"No," she said, but her voice strayed into an upper octave. "Just not something I feel like I should do right now."

He nodded, and she said, "Tell me about Three Rivers."

A measure of surprise threaded through him, but he loved the town, the ranch, all of it, and he could talk about Three Rivers forever. Before he knew it, they'd returned to Austin—and his cares and hopes about the rodeo.

———

Ethan loved finals night. He wasn't sure if any of the spectators knew what was at stake, or if they just brought their families because it was tradition, or they could get nachos, or their faces painted, or a fun and easy date night.

To him, standing under the black sky, with those bright lights shining on the arena, bordered along heaven. Add the smell of horses and manure, the roar of the crowd when someone performed well, the kiss of the wind as it lazed through the atmosphere, and Ethan couldn't remember why he'd left this life.

Standing just outside the reach of the crowd, the lights, the arena, a sense of peace enveloped him. A sense of peace so strong, Ethan closed his eyes, took a deep drag of air, and sent a prayer of gratitude toward heaven.

Here, now, in this moment, he'd found his center. He didn't have to be anyone or anything but himself, and it felt good.

Brynn's voice asking after him sent a smile skittering across his face, and he opened his eyes. She'd won earlier that evening, and because she managed to pull out wins in the bigger rodeos, she'd gone from fifth in the money winners to first.

He'd like to think she performed better for him—because he was in attendance—but his ego had already swelled to twice its normal size after his bull riding win in Montgomery. No need to add fuel to the fire.

He watched her speak with a couple of cowboys, still looking for him. The fact that she wanted to be with him coated his insides with surprise and pleasure at the same time. Someone as beautiful and successful as her usually had an equally impressive man on her arm.

His breath caught when someone finally pointed in his direction and her eyes hooked his. His fingers tingled in anticipation of touching hers, and he grinned at her as she approached.

"There you are." She stopped a few feet away, a twinge of trepidation in her expression.

"Here I am." He maintained his position against the fence. "Nice win tonight, cowgirl."

That gorgeous blush crept into her face. "You too," she said in reference to his and Tanner's team roping win. "I'll admit I don't like watching the bull riding. Makes me nervous."

He'd nearly tamped out the man he used to be, but swaggery words still popped into his mind from time to time. "So you're sayin' you're scared I might get hurt." He ducked his head and reached for her fingers, only finding the tips.

"Bulls are super dangerous," she said matter-of-factly, but she took a step closer to him. Close enough to invade his personal space.

Ethan's heart tripped for two reasons: the proximity of Brynn, and the fact that he'd be tying himself to a "super dangerous" animal in about an hour. Every time he rode a bull, his heart tried to parade out of his chest. They *were* dangerous.

"I drew Unlucky In Love." He slid his hand up her arm to her elbow. "He's on the low end of dangerous." Which meant if Ethan managed to stay on him for eight seconds, he probably wouldn't win. The difficulty factor of a handful of other bulls would ensure their riders won—if they could make it to the eight-second bell.

"Unlucky In Love?" Brynn repeated. "Let's hope that's not an omen or anything."

Ethan threw his head back and laughed. "Kiss me for luck, cowgirl. Just to be sure."

She did, and flashes of a life with Brynn stole through his mind. Flashes of the two of them, together, traveling the rodeo circuit. Flashes of a family.

He slowed his fantasies as she pulled away and whispered, "Go ride 'im, cowboy."

16

B rynn's stomach felt like someone had drilled a hole in it and then emptied a vat of acid into her veins. She couldn't seem to swallow away the nerves. Ethan's name got announced, along with, "In contention for our Rookie of the Year for bull riding," and every muscle in Brynn's body clenched.

Only Chuck sat next to her, as Daddy had gone back to the boarding house at least an hour ago. Brynn didn't think she could worry anymore than she currently was, but somehow an additional dose of anxiety flooded her when she thought about her father.

Chuck had spoken true. Daddy wasn't well.

She watched Ethan in the chute. He tightened the rope around his hand. Pounded his fist against it and tightened it further. He adjusted his legs, his spurs glinting in the light, his handsome face aglow with adrenaline and the teensiest hint of fear.

At least he was smart enough to be afraid. Brynn liked that about him. In fact, Brynn liked almost everything about Ethan.

Her tangled thoughts—*could I love him?*—vanished as he nodded at the line judge and the bell rang and the gate opened, spitting the giant, gray and white bull into the arena, Ethan on its back.

Brynn couldn't breathe watching him. He seemed to have an uncanny ability to anticipate which way the animal would throw next, and he always seemed to be leaning in the right direction.

Each second passed agonizingly slow. Her lungs burned.

Unlucky In Love dodged left.

Ethan went with him.

The bull didn't fully land before rearing again. Brynn bit down on her lip, knowing the stalled momentum would jar Ethan.

It did, but he absorbed the energy from the two-thousand-pound animal. His head snapped back, but his hat stayed on.

"Come on, come on," Brynn found herself muttering, her eyes darting from the frozen time clock to the frenzied bull thrashing around the arena.

Finally, the bell sounded. The crowd went wild, Brynn with them. Chuck laughed and clapped next to her, squeezing her in a tight hug as the celebrations died down.

A gasp went up.

Brynn's attention rocketed back to the arena. Ethan's ride had ended, but he was still on the bull. Or rather, his right hand was still attached to the bull.

Clowns swarmed the arena, some trying to pacify the bull while others attempted to help Ethan get his hand free.

A blink. A breath. Enough time to imagine the worst.

Ethan yanked his hand back again and it came free.

A triumphant yell rose from the crowd, but Brynn's vocal chords felt numb, icy. The clowns got the bull out of the arena safely, and Ethan raised both hands into the air to signal he was okay. The deafening applause didn't faze Brynn.

Look at me, look at me, she thought. Finally Ethan's eyes found hers, and he nodded to her, his mega-watt grin still in place.

She sat down just as her phone rang. She thumbed it on when she saw Daddy on the screen.

"What's up, Daddy?"

"I—" He wheezed, coughed. Clattering came through the line.

"Daddy?"

"Help," he whispered before the call ended.

Brynn stared at her phone, the iciness that had been in her throat spreading to all her extremities.

"What did he want?" Chuck asked, pulling out his own phone. "He called me too. I guess I didn't hear it because of all the excitement."

Brynn shot to her feet. "We have to go. He needs help." She reached for Chuck and started down the aisle.

"Brynn, wait—"

She spun toward him. "That's all he said. He couldn't say anything else." Her voice broke as panic and fear and anxiety roared through her. She needed to get to her father, now. "We have to go."

Chuck followed her out without another complaint. By the time they got to the boarding house, Daddy was almost blue.

Brynn stifled a scream as she ran to where he lay on the kitchen floor, his phone near his head. "Call 9-1-1!" She pressed her fingers against his throat and detected a faint pulse.

Chuck's words dulled in her ears. She couldn't see any evidence of an injury; no blood. She carefully rolled Daddy onto his back and lifted his chin by supporting his neck with her hand.

His chest rose as he drew in a breath. "Chuck," she called. "He's breathing. Has a pulse." Color reappeared in his complexion. "Daddy?" She bent close to him. "Daddy, can you hear me?"

Brynn felt like she might suffocate if he didn't respond. Tears crowded in her eyes. Her throat closed much more than, "Daddy?"

He moaned, and strong relief flowed through her.

"They're on their way," Chuck said, kneeling next to her. He checked for a pulse and picked up Daddy's phone. "Dad? Wake up, Dad."

His eyes rolled in his head, but he didn't wake. The paramedics arrived, and Brynn stepped back to let them work. Though they moved in a precise, methodical way, the urgency never left the room.

She rode in the ambulance with Daddy as Chuck followed in their truck. Brynn tried to focus on the words the paramedics said, but they flew in one ear and out the other. They wheeled him into the emergency room, and whisked him out of her sight. Chuck took care of paperwork while Brynn paced a hole in the waiting room.

Ethan burst into the hospital about twenty minutes after Daddy had disappeared behind the ER doors. He'd just gotten a new phone earlier that day, so Brynn had texted Tanner to tell him about her father. Relief that Tanner had relayed her message hit her with the force of a truck.

"Brynn." Ethan pulled her into the safety and security of his arms, and Brynn never wanted to be without his embrace again.

I love him, she thought, but so many emotions warred beneath her tongue she couldn't say more than, "Thank you for comin'."

"How is he?" He stroked the errant strands of hair off her face, smoothing his hands over her shoulders like he could put her back together with such simple motions.

"Haven't heard." The sob she'd been swallowing for the past hour climbed up her throat. "I don't even know where I'm supposed to be next." She hated that her first coherent sentence had been about the rodeo.

"Oh, don't worry 'bout that," Ethan said. "Chuck'll take care of everything."

Chuck confirmed that he indeed would take care of her rodeo career just as a doctor exited the door Brynn had been staring at.

He approached them, his eyes serious but a smile curving his mouth.

Brynn slid her arms around Ethan's waist and held on, held on.

"Your father has had a heart attack," the doctor said. Brynn didn't hear anything after that.

ANGER HAD BECOME BRYNN'S GOOD FRIEND DURING THE PAST WEEK. Fury stopped by often as well. She fumed as Chuck drove west, a horse trailer attached to the hitch.

"I don't care about Indio," Brynn finally bit out.

"I heard you the first dozen times," Chuck said.

"We should've stayed with Daddy."

"Duke's there, and they're goin' home tomorrow anyway." He glanced at her. "Nothin' you can do, Brynn."

An idea had been brewing in Brynn's head since the fateful words of "heart attack."

"I'm going to announce my retirement after the rodeo in Indio," she said.

Chuck flinched like she'd splashed icy water on him. "You are? You promised Daddy in the hospital you'd become the World Champion."

She shook her head, regret raging through her. She couldn't believe she'd said that. She was just so grateful he'd woken up, that he was expected to recover and live several more years yet.

"I've been done for a while, Chuck." Brynn stared out the passenger window so she didn't have to see her brother's face. "Don't you remember what it was like to want to retire?"

"I got hurt," he said. "I never wanted to retire."

"I'm dying," she said. "With every rodeo, I wither a little more."

"You seem happy with Ethan."

Ethan.

If there was one reason she'd stay until the season ended, it would be Ethan. Miles passed as she contemplated how to respond to Chuck. She *was* happy with Ethan. She loved having him in the stands when she rode; enjoyed watching him rope and tame bulls.

She spoke with him everyday, even though he was currently heading to Oklahoma and she to California. She'd mentioned nothing to him about her desire to quit, but she suspected he knew. He had to know. He could read her as easily as an open book—always had. He heard things in between the syllables of what she did say.

When he'd left for his next event, his parting words had been, "Hang in there, cowgirl." He punctuated the sentence with the sweetest kiss. "I'll see you in Utah."

Utah—two more months away. Brynn had to endure April and May before she'd see him again. Before she could steal his strength, mold her lips to his, tell him she was quitting and hey, maybe she loved him.

"Ethan's a dream," she muttered, not quite sure why she was letting such negativity crowd her thoughts.

"What was that?" Chuck asked.

"Nothing," Brynn said. "Absolutely nothing."

ETHAN WOKE ON SUNDAY MORNING AFTER ANOTHER BULL RIDING win. This one felt astronomically bigger than the others, because Henry Hansen had been on the ticket this time. With every ride, Ethan wanted to make his time in the rodeo more permanent. Not just a year to help Tanner, but indefinitely until he qualified for every bull ride and could reclaim his national title.

His smile seized as he thought about Brynn, miles and miles away in California. He tapped out a text to her. *How are you today?*

He wanted to ask about her event last night, but since she hadn't volunteered the information, he wouldn't.

At church came her reply.

This early?

Just sitting in the chapel.

What's goin' on?

Just thinking.

Ethan didn't know what else to say to reassure her, to cheer her, to be there for her when he wasn't physically there for her.

His thumbs tapped out three words—*I love you*—before he hurried to delete them. No way he was telling her that in a text message.

You don't even know if it's true, he told himself.

Oh, it's true, his brain argued.

And Ethan couldn't refute it.

Later that afternoon, as he toted his duffle bag down the hall and toward Tanner's truck, Henry Hansen stepped into his path.

"Hey, Greene."

"Yeah?" Ethan only half-turned back to the other cowboy.

"I'm gonna appeal last night's decision."

"You do that." Ethan flashed him a smile. He hadn't gone a rodeo without achieving the eight-second ride, and if he drew the right bull, he won. He'd ridden Only In Vegas last night, the meanest, most difficult animal in the circuit right now. Henry could appeal anything he wanted; he wasn't going to win.

"Tell your girlfriend congratulations," Henry called after him.

Against his better judgment, Ethan stalled again, the hair on the back of his neck bristling when Henry so much as spoke about Brynn. "For what?"

"Her retirement."

The air surrounding Ethan turned glacial, making his lungs stick together and his fingers tremble as he scampered away from Henry and into the safety of Tanner's truck.

He couldn't work up the nerve—or the words—to ask Tanner

if he knew about Brynn's retirement. As they headed to another rodeo in another town, Ethan's anger rallied.

When they stopped for dinner, he asked, "Did you know Brynn retired?"

Tanner barely glanced at him. "Yeah. It was on the news this morning." He got out of the truck but peered back in. "You didn't know?"

Ethan's mood darkened. "Henry told me as we were leavin'."

"This is why you should watch more TV." Tanner shrugged. "You comin'?"

"No," Ethan said. "Leave me the keys so I don't roast in here. I need to make a phone call." He dialed Brynn at the same time he restarted Tanner's truck.

"Hey," she answered. She didn't sound different. Not timid. Or afraid. Or free. Just the same, pretty little Brynn.

"Hey," he said. "You retired?"

"Yeah, I—"

"And I had to hear about it from Henry Hansen?" The anger Ethan had been tempering for hours rose through his throat. "Why didn't you tell me?"

"I guess I should've told you first."

"You *guess* you should've told me before telling the whole country?"

"I—I don't know what you want me to say. It's my career, and it's not like we've talked about—"

"I want to talk with you about everything," he interrupted. "I want to know what's going on in your life. I want to help you if I can." He took a deep breath and tried to add a note of compassion to his tone. "You don't have to do everything alone, Brynn."

"You're in Nebraska."

"And we're talkin' just fine."

"I'm sorry." She stated it explicitly, and it sounded true. He ached to be wherever she was, so he could hold her and kiss her and comfort her.

He exhaled, most of his anger going with the air. "I really don't like Henry Hansen."

She giggled, which released the dam in his throat. He chuckled, and soon she'd told him everything about her father, and why she'd decided to retire.

"I've been wanting to for a while," she said. "Remember when I said I was tired the first time we met?"

"I remember." Ethan didn't tell her he remembered everything they'd talked about, everything about her. "I just didn't know you were seriously considering quitting."

"It's technically a retirement for my daddy's health reasons."

The playful tone of her voice coaxed a smile from him. "I have to finish out the year. I can't abandon Tanner now."

"I know," she said. "I'm done in California, and Chuck and I are headed back to Colorado Springs. Maybe I could meet you somewhere, at one of your events."

"We were gonna meet up in Spanish Fork, remember?" he said. "It's quite a drive to Utah from Colorado Springs, but that might be the closest one for a while."

"That's not 'till June." The depressed nature of her voice lifted his spirits.

"Are you sayin' you miss me?"

"Only if you say it first," she teased.

"Oh, I'm missin' you bad, cowgirl."

"I miss you too." Her serious, emotion-filled words encouraged Ethan, sent shivers down his back, almost made him tell her he loved her.

He clamped his lips around the words. He wanted to tell her in person, when he could see her eyes and judge her reaction and kiss her afterward. "Utah, then."

"Utah," she confirmed. Ethan hung up reassured, but with snakes of worry writhing through his guts, his fantasies of traveling on the rodeo circuit with Brynn in pieces at his feet.

She'd quit right when he wanted to stay.

What do I do now, Lord? he prayed. *I'm not in Colorado anymore. So what do I do now?*

The sermon the pastor had given months ago—in Colorado —flashed through his mind. *Let the Lord help you.*

"Okay." He sighed as he got out of the truck. "Help me...." He didn't even know how to finish the sentence, because he needed help with so many things.

FOR THE FIRST TIME, ETHAN WISHED HE COULD CROSS OUT DAYS ON this phone's calendar app. But he couldn't, so he took to swiping through the weeks, counting each one, until he'd see Brynn again. First it took eight swipes—eight weeks.

Then seven.

Then six.

Everywhere he went, the announcers talked and talked about him. He'd been sitting at the top of the money board for bull riding since he'd beaten Henry. He became more and more like Brynn—and less and less like the rider he'd been last time he was in the rodeo circuit—by eating on the fringes of the cities where he stayed, by showing up at the last minute and leaving right after the event's awards.

Five, four, three, two swipes until he'd see Brynn. He'd forgotten what she smelled like, what the shape of her hand felt like in his. He retained the quality of her voice, because they had a weekly Sunday phone call.

By the time he arrived in Utah, he hadn't heard from or talked to Brynn in a few days. He wasn't sure what he was more nervous about—seeing her after nine weeks apart, or riding a bull. Every female voice made him check over his shoulder, hoping it would be her. Tanner glared his face off in the hours leading up the team roping, and Ethan heard the silent lecture pouring from his eyes.

Focus.

If only he could. His skin tingled to touch Brynn's. He licked his lips and pulled himself together as tightly as he could. When the pair exited the stadium to deafening applause and the second highest score of the night, Ethan wanted to give Tanner's glare right back to him.

But he didn't. Instead, he spent the hour between events desperately looking for Brynn. He couldn't find her.

She hadn't come.

Despair swept through him, lodging behind his lungs and making breathing difficult. Why hadn't she come?

He pulled his phone out to see if she'd called or texted. Surely she'd have known she couldn't meet him by that morning, as it took almost eight hours to drive from Colorado Springs.

His phone showed him nothing.

He stared into the night sky, the beautiful Rocky Mountains nearly glowing in the purple sunset. His mind almost seemed frozen, unable to work.

"Ethan!" Tanner called.

Ethan snapped out of the funk, turning as if encased in quicksand toward the voice.

"You're on in thirty." Tanner hooked his thumb down the arena. "C'mon. You drew Ready to Roll. You've got to get ready to roll."

Somehow, Ethan got his feet to take him in the direction Tanner wanted him, that burning question leaving holes in his mind.

Why hadn't Brynn come?

17

Brynn stepped out of her house on Thursday morning and took a deep, deep, deep breath. She couldn't get enough of the air in Three Rivers. She'd been in town for a month, and she finally felt like the rental she'd secured on an hour's notice was clean. No one had lived in the two-bedroom home for a couple of years, and the inches of dust had testified of it.

She looked up into the baby blue sky, the birds chirping in the stand of trees to her right. *Help Ethan tonight*, she sent to the Lord. It was only the first day of the rodeo, but she knew by his silence that he wasn't happy she couldn't join him in Utah.

She hadn't explained why either, choosing to tell him she simply "couldn't make the drive" via text than over the phone. She wanted her existence in Three Rivers to be a surprise. A welcome home gift.

Turning, she re-entered the house and went over her proposal one more time. The delivery was flawless—not too desperate, not too arrogant. She'd spent her time in Three Rivers wandering the quaint little town, familiarizing herself with the people, the pastor, the paths in and out of the city.

"You've got this," she whispered to herself as she closed her folder. Forty-five minutes later, she arrived at Three Rivers Ranch for at least the fifteenth time. She'd been out to the barns, the therapeutic riding facilities, the outbuildings. She'd taken measurements, and researched local laws about how many structures could exist in a certain space, and met with the owner of the ranch, Squire Ackerman.

She'd meet with him again today, her final proposal in hand. He and the owner of Courage Reins, Pete Marshall, had been more than accommodating, if not a bit leery of her idea to start a champion horse training facility at Three Rivers.

Brynn swallowed, her nerves crowding her throat again. Just like they had the first time she showed up at Three Rivers to recruit Ethan. Just as they had when she came the second time to give her initial proposal.

Another deep breath, another prayer—this one for the Lord's help in making this proposal into a reality—and Brynn strode down the dirt road that led to the administration trailer. Up the steps, through the door. Brynn coached herself to breathe.

"Mornin'," Howie, the general controller, said from behind his desk. She'd learned that Ethan used to sit at that desk, run this ranch. The knowledge only made her admire him more. "Squire's waitin' for ya in his office."

"Thanks." She flashed him the warmest smile she could manage and turned to head down the aisle. A few cowboys passed her as she went, tipping their hats in her direction. Ethan had been right. The cowboys at Three Rivers were different. Kinder. Stronger in ways that mattered. Dutiful. Hardworking.

Every time she came to the ranch, it didn't matter who she ran into. They could help her, always with a quick smile and a respectful tip of the hat.

Brynn heard two male voices in Squire's office, and she paused. Her well-practiced speech fled. The folder in her fist got crushed.

She forced herself to keep going, to enter the office, and shake the military men's hands. They towered over her, much the same way Ethan did, but they carried compassion in their expressions too.

"All right," Squire said. "Lay it on us." He exchanged a glance with Pete, who kept his penetrating green eyes on Brynn.

"All right," she echoed as she flipped open the folder. Strength flowed back into her, lifting her voice and edging it with enthusiasm as she said, "Bowman's Champion Breeds will need ten acres of land, with training facilities for barrel racing, team roping, and bronc riding." She flipped a page which showed the professional logo she'd had designed. "This goes nicely with what Courage Reins already uses." She nodded to Pete. "And incorporates the general family feel of Three Rivers Ranch."

She took a moment to breathe, to swallow. "I know y'all were concerned about the traffic my horse trainin' would bring, and I had a study done." She slid them each a piece of yellow paper. "The traffic increase would be minimal—sixty-three percent less than what Courage Reins is causing—and during the fall and winter months, when rodeo riders are lookin' for new animals for the upcoming season."

A flash of pride stole through Brynn as she watched Squire and Pete examine her traffic study. They set the papers down in a near-synchronized fashion, and a smile spread her lips. "I love Three Rivers. I love the town. I love this ranch. I love—" Emotion caught in her throat, and for some reason she couldn't fathom, her thoughts flew to Ethan.

"I love training horses," she finished as she turned another page. "I can offer this amount for the land. I'd hire out my own construction. I know people in the horse business—maybe I can find you an excellent therapy horse, or get a good deal on a workin' horse for the ranch." She sat back, her presentation nearly over. "I think I'd be a real great addition to this ranch, and I want this more than anything."

Squire leaned over the desk and took the paper with her offer on it. He whistled, real low, and handed it to Pete.

"I'm already in," Pete said without looking at the number. He glanced at Squire. "I like her. Haven't I always said I liked her?"

"Yeah, you have." Squire wore a smile in his voice, but it didn't touch his face. He leaned back in his chair, his strong arms crossed. "Can I call you tomorrow and let you know?"

"What's to—?"

Squire silenced Pete with a well-daggered look. When he met Brynn's eye again, he'd softened it.

"Tomorrow's fine," she said. "I'll leave that with you." She stood, shook both men's hands, and held her head high as she left the building.

Once in the safety of her car, her stomach rioted against her. Her head pounded. Her heart throbbed. Had she done enough to make her dream come true?

Most of all, she couldn't wait to call Ethan that evening and find out how he did at the rodeo. Couldn't wait to tell him that she had everything worked out for them to be together. With a training facility at Three Rivers, he could have the two things he loved in one place.

ETHAN BARELY HUNG ONTO HIS TEMPER, BARELY HUNG ONTO THE questions he had, barely hung on until the eight-second bell sounded. As soon as it did, he jumped down and hopped on the fence. Another jump and he got over, his fingers already itchin' to get to his phone so he could call Brynn.

"Don't you want to see who wins this heat?" Tanner asked, coming up alongside him.

"Don't care," Ethan said. "I qualified. I'll be back tomorrow." He left Tanner standing in the middle the road, his thoughts singular.

By the time he got his gear and got out of the arena, the sick feeling he'd had when he'd heard Brynn say she didn't like cowboys waged war with his chest cavity. He dialed her even though she was an hour ahead of him. Surely she'd be up.

"Ethan!" Her excited voice battled with the negative feeling roiling inside him.

"Hey." His voice sounded like someone had roped his neck and pulled too tight.

"How'd you—?"

"Why aren't you here?"

Gallons of silence poured through the line. Too much. Ethan suddenly didn't want to know. "Look," he said. "We've got to work on your communication skills."

"Wait, what? *My* communication skills? What are you talkin' about?"

As much as he wished he could be someone different, he couldn't. He was still the old, jealous, quick-tempered Ethan Greene. The one he'd been trying to tame for the past year and a half. The one who'd tried something different with Brynn and succeeded.

His gut dropped to his boots as the swirling, maddening, consuming thoughts gelled inside his mind. "You're datin' someone else."

"I am not."

"Did you forget we were meetin' in Utah this weekend?"

"Of course I didn't. I texted you, like, seven times about why I couldn't make it."

Ethan shook his head, his jaw tightening with each movement. "No. I never got a text from you."

"I'll send you a screen shot."

"I don't need a screen shot!"

An intake of breath came through the line. "Okay, I'm gonna hang up," Brynn said. "*I* did text you about not coming. *I* apologized a bunch of times. *You* never responded."

"I didn't—" But Ethan didn't finish. She'd hung up.

Brynn made his blood boil, in more ways than one.

Why are you so angry with her? he asked himself.

I want to see her!

So you can yell at her some more?

No, so I— He cut off the thought, knowing where it would take him. He wanted to see Brynn. Hold her. Smell her. Kiss her.

Tell her he loved her.

He'd been planning their reunion for eight solid weeks, and he felt like it had been stolen from him. Robbed right out from under him, without warning.

Maybe she did text you.

He sighed and leaned against the window in the truck. Maybe she'd texted. Maybe she hadn't. Maybe she was dating someone new in Colorado Springs. Maybe she wasn't.

"Doesn't matter now," he told himself as he flipped the truck into gear and peeled out of the parking lot. "Your old temper just ruined things with her."

But he knew it wasn't his temper that had ruined things. It was him.

Him.

The good, calm, patient Ethan he couldn't quite grasp, the man he wanted to be so badly, the one who slipped away from him like smoke through his fingers whenever things got hard.

ETHAN SUFFERED THROUGH DAYS, WEEKS, MONTHS OF RODEO. Without Brynn to speak with every week, without the promise of seeing her, without anyone but Tanner for company, the rodeo held the same drudgery it had previously.

"When are you gonna stop mopin' around?" Tanner asked one morning in October. "You realize you're the big money winner in bull riding this year, right?" He threw back a swig of coffee. "I don't understand you."

"I don't understand me either." Ethan threw Tanner a murderous glare, wishing he wasn't on the leaderboard. If he wasn't, that would mean his rodeo season had ended. As it was, he and Tanner were on the ticket for the National Finals Rodeo for team roping. And he needed to get ready to compete for the Rookie of the Year award in bull riding.

Two more months, he told himself.

Problem was, in two months, he didn't know what to do next. He did like winning, and the money he'd earned this past ten months was more than he'd earn in five years workin' at Three Rivers Ranch.

Still, the thought of the ranch called to him. Sang to his soul.

At the same time, he wasn't sure he should walk away from the rodeo so quickly. Didn't want to repeat the same mistakes. Mistakes he should've learned from the first time.

"Maybe I should just call her," he mumbled into his omelet, because it was his birthday and he wanted to hear her voice. It would be the best gift he could get.

Tanner's head jerked up, his attention finally off his phone. "Call who?" he asked carefully.

"You know who." Ethan hadn't spoken Brynn's name in months. Thought about her everyday, yes. Fantasized about holding her and making things right, sure. But actually speaking to her, or about her? Another of his flaws—his pride—didn't allow it.

"She was a huge distraction." Tanner went back to his phone. "You've won twice as much since she—you...broke up."

Ethan heard something in Tanner's tone. He peered at his friend and roping partner, but the other man stayed fixated on his phone.

"Why'd you guys break up?" Ethan asked. He'd been curious about Tanner and Brynn's relationship since day one, but had been satisfied with Brynn's explanation. The temperate part of him—the man he was trying to be—had pushed away the remaining curiosity.

"Like I said, she was a distraction." He flipped his phone over and sat back from his empty plate. "Brynn likes to be first. She's used to it. And with me, she'd never be first." He jabbed one finger at Ethan. "You either. Trust me. It's better this way."

The massive hole in Ethan's heart, in his life, told a different story. "I—She was first for me. I'm only doin' this for you."

Instead of gratitude or compassion or any of the other emotions Ethan would expect Tanner to show, he only saw fear flow across his partner's face. Confused, Ethan cocked his head. "You know I'm only still here because of you, right?"

"Yeah, I know." Tanner picked up his phone. "But I thought you'd join up next year too. I mean, you've said so a coupla times."

Ethan gazed out the window behind Tanner. He had said he was thinking about coming back to rodeo. But then Brynn had quit, and Ethan's plans to head on back to Three Rivers came roaring back. Since June, though, he couldn't settle on any plans. Which actually suited the old Ethan just fine. He lived day to day, minute to minute, without cares or worries about the future.

He'd been trying to just get by, but sitting there, in a hotel breakfast room in Arizona, Ethan realized he needed to make a choice.

Try again to become the man he wanted to be for Brynn. Find her, apologize, tell her how he felt.

Or join the rodeo circuit and embrace the man he'd once been.

"Well, let's go," Tanner said. "Those ropes don't throw themselves."

Ethan got up and followed him out, the familiar *two more months* rotating through his head. But now he knew he only had to endure eight more weeks without Brynn.

18

Brynn had three nails in her mouth and one in the roof of her new stables, a hammer poised to knock it home, when her phone buzzed in her back pocket. The vibrations startled her, and she almost brought the hammer down on her thumb.

She wiped sweat—October in Texas was no joke—from beneath the brim of her hat and laid the tool on the plywood. Down from her, Brett Murphy, the best recommended contractor in two states continued positioning boards and nailing them into place.

Brynn checked the screen and almost fell off the roof at the sight of Ethan's face. She should've purged his number from her contacts eons ago. But she hadn't been able to. Didn't want to admit that she wouldn't get to hear from him again.

In the back of her mind, she knew he'd come back to Three Rivers eventually. She wasn't sure if it would be after the National Finals Rodeo, which he'd qualified for in both his events, or later, after he'd become a rodeo superstar again.

She'd prepared herself for the day he returned, no matter when it was. Squire had sold her the land, but he and Pete had insisted she hire Brett to build her training grounds as part of the deal. He'd brought his whole family from North Carolina, and they'd rented a house in town for a while.

"I'm not movin' back permanently," Brett had growled on more than one occasion. "I have a business at the estate."

But Brynn had seen how far Three Rivers had sunk its teeth into both Brett and his wife, Kate. The town—the very air in Texas—had a way of doing that.

Despite Ethan's long silence and strange break-up with her—she *had* texted him about her absence in Utah. Five times, to be exact. She had taken a screen shot, though she didn't dare send it to him. She'd never heard the level of fury in his voice before he'd yelled at her over the phone.

She took so long to think about what he wanted now, all these months later, that the call ended before she could answer. *It's just as well*, she told herself as she picked up the hammer. She'd seen him on TV lots of times. Couldn't seem to stop herself from watching. And she'd seen him with cowgirls draped over both arms. She'd re-implemented her no-cowboy rule and managed to keep it, though cowboys surrounded her these days.

Her phone vibrated once, the signal that she had a new voice-mail message. She toyed with the idea of deleting it unheard as she worked through the morning. By lunchtime, they'd completed the roof.

"I've never seen a woman do what you do," Brett said as he waited for her at the bottom of the ladder.

"I don't know if that's a compliment or not." Brynn pulled off her gloves and tucked them in her back pocket.

"It is." He slid her a grin and nodded toward something behind her. "I think Aaron would say so too."

Brynn glanced at the lingering cowhand, her heart suddenly cold around the edges. "Just tryin' to help."

"You're handy," Brett said. "I should hire you to come work for me."

She laughed. "I'm desperate to get this place open by Christmas. That doesn't mean I'm handy."

"It'll be done by the holidays, Miss Brynn," Brett promised. "Now, let's go eat. This heat is killin' me."

Several things were slowly killing Brynn, including the bull rider-sized hole in her life. But she tucked her arm into Brett's and entered the blessed air conditioning in the Courage Reins headquarters, where Reese, the facilitator of the company, had lunch set up in the conference room.

ETHAN DIDN'T TRY TO CALL BRYNN AGAIN AFTER THE SILENCE HE'D gotten for his birthday. His message had gone unreturned. Quick fire licked his insides whenever he considered that she hadn't even listened to it.

He went back to church, looking for answers and help and anything he could to submerge the man he didn't want to be. He'd decided to be the better man. Now he just had to work at it until he became that person. He'd try Brynn again then.

Selfish as he was, he prayed every night that she was happy, but not dating anyone. Begged God to give him time to be the man she deserved. Asked for blessings he probably didn't deserve, but wanted anyway.

He ate Thanksgiving dinner with his mother, being in the same city as Brynn and not seeing her almost more than he could stand. He nearly drove by her house a hundred times, but kept himself from doing it. He hadn't spoken to her brothers or her father either. Guilt needled him—her father had suffered a heart attack. Ethan should at least stop by and see how he was doing. He didn't.

The next day he joined Tanner in his king cab truck for the long drive to Las Vegas. The miles rolled by, the scenery gradually changing from a snow-kissed mountain to a dry desert. Tanner had found them somewhere quiet, on the outskirts of the city, to stay. They took the horses to the barn, got them settled in, before he said, "Two more weeks."

He looked at the desert sky like it would grant him the championship he wanted.

"Yeah," Ethan said.

"You make a decision about next year yet?" Tanner asked.

Ethan exhaled. He hadn't been able to tell Tanner his plans. He'd held off on making any, just trying to listen and do what God wanted him to.

"Yeah," Ethan said. "I'm not gonna come back."

Tanner swore, his expression turning stormy. "Why not? Ethan, you're good. Really good."

"It's just not for me." Ethan tucked his hands in his pockets, a blip of fear running through him at the fury in Tanner's eyes. The rodeo definitely wasn't for the man Ethan was trying to become, and he knew it. His soul ached to return to the range, to the simple life of branding cattle and filling troughs with water and brushing down horses. To working good, solid earth, and laughing with other cowhands, and trying to find the right woman in a small, country town.

"Is it because of Brynn?"

Ethan flinched at the sound of her name. "No. She won't even call me back."

Triumph flashed across Tanner's face. "She's stubborn like that."

Her stubbornness made Ethan smile. "Yeah, she is."

"You're still in love with her." Disbelief carried in Tanner's voice.

"Nah." Ethan glanced down and scuffed his feet in the dirt.

"You are." Tanner stalked closer. "I can't believe this! Even after all she's done. Won't return your phone calls. Didn't tell you she wasn't coming to Utah. Only thought of herself at every rodeo." He ticked her heinous actions off on his fingers, one by one.

Ethan's temper rose, and he lifted his gaze to Tanner's, a measure of the same fire flowing through him. "She said she texted about Utah." Over the past two months as Ethan sat in church, he'd forgiven Brynn. He had no other choice, and it had been freeing and wonderful. And if she'd forgive him, he'd take her back in a second.

"Of course she'd say that!" Tanner yelled.

"I can't spend the rest of my life being mad about it," Ethan said. "I forgave her."

Tanner scoffed, threw his hands in the air, and paced away. "You forgave her. Of course you did. The God-fearing bull rider."

Ethan's lungs seized. "What's that supposed to mean?"

"Will you forgive me, then?" Tanner took a step closer, and Ethan fell back a pace, unsettled by the dangerous glint in his eye.

"For what?"

"Erasing her texts. The ones tellin' you that she wouldn't make it to Utah."

His words landed like bombs in Ethan's ears. The sky seemed to crumble under the weight of what he'd said.

"You mean, you—"

"Yeah, me." Tanner thumped his chest. "She's a huge distraction, and I needed you to focus. So I did what I had to do."

Fury like Ethan had never known roared through him. "I've been miserable for months."

"Boo hoo," Tanner sneered. "You've won more money in those months than you'll make in years at that pathetic ranch."

Ethan studied the horizon, his heart beating a million miles an hour. His mind spun just as fast. "She texted me. She told me." He shook his head as Tanner said something that didn't register.

"I've been so stupid." Ethan spun and sprinted toward Tanner's truck, the other man's shouts blurring into the surroundings. All Ethan could hear was *Get to Brynn. Get to Brynn now.*

ETHAN RANG THE DOORBELL AGAIN, PUNCTUATED THE ACTION WITH several loud bangs to Brynn's front door. He didn't care that it was after eleven o'clock at night. He'd taken the first flight he could and nearly lost his mind waiting in the line to rent a car.

"C'mon." He peered in the dark window alongside the door. He pounded again. Finally, a light flared to life, and he caught someone shuffling toward the door.

"What in—? Ethan?" Chuck stood behind the screen, a baseball bat clutched in one hand. "What are you doin'?"

"I need to talk to Brynn."

"Well, goodie for you." He scowled as he unlocked and pushed open the screen door. "Get in here. It's ten below freezing out there."

Ethan stepped across the threshold into warmth. "Is she awake?"

"I wouldn't know. She doesn't live here anymore."

Ethan's heart burst right out of his chest, zoomed around the room, and barreled back into place. "What?"

"She moved to Three Rivers 'bout six months ago."

"Three Rivers?" Ethan couldn't make anything line up. Maybe he was more tired than he thought. Maybe he needed to lie down.

"Yeah." Chuck leaned against the back of the couch, arms folded, and studied Ethan. "Said that if you ever came here lookin' for her, to tell you she went to Three Rivers. Nothin' more, nothin' less."

"What's she doin' there?"

Chuck shrugged, though by the smirk riding his lips, the little devil knew exactly what Brynn was doing in Three Rivers.

"Chuck...."

"Brynn told me what to tell you. I told you. Can I go back to bed now?"

"Three Rivers," Ethan muttered, thinking of another six hours until he could see Brynn. And not just six, as he couldn't go beating down her door at five o'clock in the morning.

"Look, why don't you crash here tonight?" Chuck patted the couch. "Get up nice and early to make the drive. Catch her right about lunchtime, when she's sure to be in a good mood."

Ethan looked at the couch, then at Chuck. "You really won't tell me anything else?"

"Do you think I want to get punched next time I see my sister?" Chuck chuckled. "See you in the mornin', Ethan." He turned and went down the hall.

Ethan collapsed on the couch, knowing full-well he couldn't safely make the drive to Three Rivers that night. He lay down, intending to sleep for just a couple of hours. Then he'd get to see Brynn, tell her how sorry and stupid and silly he'd been. Hold her. Breathe her into his soul. Tell her he loved her.

Soon, he promised as he drifted into unconsciousness.

19

Brynn sat by herself on the pew in the back corner. The choir sang Christmas hymns, even though it was only the first week of December. The corners of her lips turned up on their own accord with the songs of the Savior.

With any luck, her training facilities would be done by Christmas. As the music drifted into silence, she bowed her head and thanked the Lord for all He'd helped her with over the past several months.

Pastor Scott started to speak, his message clear in his opening statement, "God is good, my friends."

Brynn couldn't agree more, though she wished she had a certain someone sitting next to her, holding her hand, pressing his lips to her temple, she couldn't argue with the pastor. God had been good to her.

Something nagged at her, something that had been niggling in her mind for a couple of months. She needed to move past Ethan, and in order to do that, she needed to listen to his message —and probably call him back.

Curiosity sank through her, as it had everyday since he'd called. *Today*, she told herself. She'd listen to the message and move on today. She deserved the peace that would come with closure, and Ethan did too.

After the services ended, Brynn slipped out the doors at the front of the pack, the way she usually did. She'd been able to buy her house and get to know a few neighbors in the half-year she'd lived in Three Rivers, but she still didn't want to stick around for the after-church gossip the ladies at the ranch had warned her about. They often invited her to sit with them and their families, but Brynn enjoyed the solace of her solo worship.

At home, she barricaded herself in the safety of her bedroom and swiped her phone to life. With the voicemail open, she finally allowed herself to press the play button.

"Hey, Brynn. It's Ethan. I'm sure you've deleted my number from your phone by now, and wow, that hurts more than I thought it would." He exhaled, and she imagined his crystal blue eyes contemplating the sky as he thought about what to say next.

"It's my birthday today, and I guess I'm being selfish, but the only thing I want is to hear your voice. Maybe you could call me back?" The hope in his voice pierced her right through the heart.

The message ended, and a tear dripped off the end of Brynn's nose. He'd called her on his birthday, and she'd ignored him. She hadn't known, but still.

She hated the heat in her head that came with crying. But cry, she did. She cried because she'd missed his birthday. She cried because she should've called him back and given him what he wanted. She cried because she was still in love with Ethan Greene, and she didn't want to let him go.

ETHAN PARKED IN FRONT OF THE BURNT ORANGE HOUSE, HIS PULSE thrumming through his entire body. According to Squire, Brynn lived in this house.

The garage sat closed, the yard neat and trim, the trees unconcerned by his presence. He killed the engine in his rental and climbed out. He wiped his hands on his jeans as he made his way toward the front door.

He'd slept later than he intended, then had to wait for someone on the ranch to get home from church so he could find out where she was.

With the hour he'd spent at Three Rivers Ranch, he'd figured out what she'd been doing here. The large, well-designed sign on the barn had been a dead giveaway. Bowman's Champion Breeds.

Ethan had never smiled so wide. She'd figured out what to do —something she was passionate about.

His heart had been aching since Tanner had admitted he'd deleted her texts, but standing out on the ranch he loved, Ethan felt like it might burst from wanting. From wanting to be with Brynn on that ranch, working with her to train those horses. From wanting to know what to do with his life, the way she seemingly had figured out.

"You gonna stand on my front lawn all afternoon?"

His gaze flew to the porch, where Brynn in all her beautiful glory stood. He didn't think. He swooped up the stairs and took her in his arms, relieved and surprised when she actually let him. "I'm sorry," he breathed into her ear. "Please forgive me."

He put a bit of distance between them so he could see her chocolatey eyes, but kept his hands anchored to her waist. "I am in love with you, Brynn Bowman." The desire to kiss her tripled when he found the same emotion in her expression.

"I've loved you for months and months," he continued, encouraged by the way her bottom lip shook and her hands slid up his chest and snaked around his neck. "And I'm so sorry I let something as stupid as a text get between us. I was foolish, and tired, and confused, and—I hate the rodeo. I hate the person I am when I ride and rope, and I hate that I let it—"

"Oh, kiss me already."

Ethan didn't have to decide if he should or not. Didn't have to wonder if he was being the right person by kissing her.

Kissing her made him the man he wanted to be. So kiss her he did.

LATER THAT NIGHT, HE LAY WITH HER IN THE HAMMOCK SHE'D PUT in the huge tree in her backyard. She curled into him, and he played with the ends of her hair.

"So, we should talk about Vegas," she said.

"Please don't."

"You have to go back. You could win."

"I don't care about winning."

"I've heard you say differently before."

Ethan pressed his teeth together. "Brynn—"

She lifted herself up, but the hammock built for one didn't allow her to hold the position. She slipped back into his side. "Ethan, it's one more rodeo. I'll come watch you win."

His hopes lifted toward the clouds, but he shook his head. "You're better than any eight second ride."

"Ethan, I—"

"I already asked Squire for my job back. My cabin is still empty. I don't care about the rodeo." And he didn't, not really. At the same time, a twinge of guilt at leaving Tanner in the lurch threaded through him. Despite what he'd done, Tanner deserved to have an opportunity to defend his championship.

And with that thought, Ethan knew he'd become the man he wanted to be. One who could forgive, and love, and choose to do the right things.

"I wasn't going to argue about the rodeo," Brynn said, her voice on the huffy side.

"No? What were you gonna say, then?"

"Well, I don't want to say it now."

He slipped his fingers from her arm to her ribs. "C'mon, cowgirl. Tell me."

She giggled as he tickled her. "Stop it." She laughed and squirmed, her leg sliding over his. "I mean it, Ethan. Stop."

He laughed with her and moved his hand back to the safer spot on her upper arm.

She tilted her head back and looked at him. "I love you," she said.

Ethan's heart filled and filled, the hole in his life vanishing completely with her statement. He slid down in the hammock so he could kiss her, but she ducked her head.

"But I'm not lettin' you kiss me until you agree to go back to Las Vegas."

"Brynn."

"Ethan."

He sighed, defeated already, though he wanted to argue. "Fine. I'll go back to Vegas. Can I kiss you now?"

She slid her arm around his back, tilting him into her. "No. *I'm* going to kiss you."

ETHAN PULLED THE ROPE AROUND HIS PALM TIGHTER, TIGHTER still. The arena seemed four times as big as any he'd competed in previously. But Brynn sat in the front row on the opposite end of the stands.

He steadfastly kept his concentration on the two-ton animal beneath him, the quality of his preparation. He'd drawn the second toughest bull in the draw: Turns On A Dime. He'd need every ounce of concentration to pull out a win, especially because Henry Hansen had drawn Only In Vegas, the bull with the highest scoring index.

Ethan closed his eyes and counted to eight, breathing through each second.

One more ride, he thought. *Help me through one more ride, Lord.*

His eyes snapped open, and the bright lights and loud crowd threatened to unseat his focus.

"Ready?" the chute holder yelled, his face earnest. "Ready?"

Ethan nodded, quick shakes of his head, and the gate opened. The bull lurched.

1...

Ethan got thrown left, but managed to balance himself with his arm.

2...

The crowd blurred into blackness, his focus on the tiny shifts of the bull beneath him.

3...

His legs tensed as he slid a tiny bit sideways, as the bull seemed to know—and bolted the opposite way.

4...

Ethan tightened every muscle in his body, countered with his arm, gripped with his boots. Stayed on.

5...

His neck snapped back as the bull reared, as the animal roared with frustration.

6...

The bull landed, barely long enough to push off again, before twisting right. Ethan went with him, had anticipated the movement.

7...

With his ride one second away from winning, Ethan allowed his weight to settle in his boots as the bull dove down.

8...

Turns On A Dime snarled, kicked, and Ethan felt completely in control as the bell sounded.

All at once, the crowd returned, the lights blared, the bull snorted. He released his tight grip on the rope and leapt from the beast's back as the clowns swarmed the field.

The bull got rushed out of the arena, but Ethan stood in the soft dirt, both hands raised above his head. He waved to the crowd as the announcer bellowed for them to give him a rousing goodbye.

He locked eyes with Brynn, who wore a giant smile and applauded him along with everyone else.

His adrenaline stayed high through the other rides, with two more rookies completing their eight-second rides. Once again, he didn't possess the self-control Brynn did, and he glanced up at the jumbo-tron to see if he'd won.

He had.

Ethan's chest expanded as gratitude filled him. He offered a prayer of thanks while the announcer went through the other four top money winners.

"And give it up for Ethan Greene, your Rookie of the Year champion!"

JULY FOURTH

"Time to eat!" Kelly Ackerman called from the deck. The football game in the backyard broke down, and Brynn watched as Ethan scooped Brett's little girl onto his shoulders, smiled as the three-year-old squealed and laughed, turned as Chelsea put her arm around Brynn's shoulder.

"He ask you to marry him yet?"

"Nope," Kelly answered for her as the men and kids reached the bottom of the stairs. "No diamond."

Brynn smiled at the women she'd come to love. She'd never had girlfriends before, but Kelly and Chelsea—and Juliette as she came out of the house with her little boy asleep on her shoulder—had become her friends and confidantes over the past several months.

"I shouldn't have said anything," Brynn said.

"Yes, you should. The man should propose." Chelsea pinned Ethan with a glare as he arrived on the deck.

"Shh," Brynn warned. "He's—"

"Who's hungry?" Kelly yelled over her. "We've got potato salad, fried chicken, ribs, that frog eye stuff Reese loves." She made a face at the limping cowboy who brought up the rear of the group with his wife, Carly, as everyone gathered around the two six-foot tables set up on the deck. They practically bent under the weight of the food Brynn had helped prepare.

"I'll take that home with me," Reese said, his dark eyes glittering like black diamonds. Brynn adored him, the quiet way he and Carly took care of everything and everyone—including her.

Ethan slid his arm around Brynn's waist and they lingered on the edge of the crowd. Kelly finished explaining the food just as a blue SUV came down the lane, kicking a trail of dust into the heated July air.

"Tom's here," Garth announced. "I'll take 'im." He took the sleeping child from his wife and she flew down the steps to greet the couple as they got out of the car.

"He's her nephew," Ethan said by way of explanation. "Tom and Rose live in Montana. He now works the ranch he grew up on."

"Ah." Brynn watched as a girl about thirteen years old got out of the backseat, and Tom hugged his aunt, and Rose put her arm around the girl.

"That's Rose's daughter, Mari," Ethan said. "She used to be one of our clients at Courage Reins."

Brynn nodded, suddenly glad there were more people here who'd also been out of the scene at Three Rivers.

"I'm so glad you came," Garth said to Rose as he squeezed her shoulders.

Tom clapped Squire and then Pete on the back, his grin as wide as the state he was visiting.

"Let's pray," Kelly said as people started talking again. "Then we can catch up." She grinned at everyone, the hint of tears in her eyes. She stretched up on her toes and said something to Squire, who smiled and pressed a kiss to her cheek.

He bent his head and said grace, and a keen sense of belonging careened through Brynn. She'd been at Three Rivers for just over a year, and with Kelly and Chelsea and Kate and

Rose and Juliette and Carly, she felt like she had sisters she'd never enjoyed. Relationships with people who loved her, encouraged her to keep trying, cheered her when she failed.

Ethan fell into line behind her, and they waited behind the kids and moms balancing more than one plate.

"I have somethin' to ask you," Ethan said, his voice low beneath all the chatter and laughter.

She picked up a paper plate. "All right."

"Will you marry me?"

A diamond ring dropped onto her plate, right where she'd been about to place a large dollop of potato salad.

She shrieked, which effectively silenced the conversation and brought every eye to her. She dropped the spoon of potato salad back into the bowl, barely able to hold onto the plate.

"You're askin' me to marry you right now?"

"Well, we don't have to get married right this second, no." Ethan glanced around at the group, obviously perplexed.

Brynn's heart galloped the way she spurred her horses to do. She didn't know what to say.

"At least try it on." Ethan picked up the ring. "Carly said it would fit you."

"Carly—" Brynn locked her eyes on the woman who had become her best friend. "You sneak. You said he hadn't bought a ring yet."

"I didn't want to spoil the surprise." She leaned into Reese, a grin on her face.

"I knew it," Ethan said, glancing around. "Y'all can't keep your noses out of anything. How long have you been talkin' about when I was gonna ask her?"

"Weeks," Kelly said at the same time Chelsea said, "Only a few days," at the same time Squire said, "'Bout a year."

Brynn burst into laughter, though a trickle of tears threatened to escape. Ethan slid the ring on her finger, effectively silencing her. "Looks nice." He peered at her. "So? You wanna get married, cowgirl?"

"Of course I do." She threw her arms around him, basking in the strength of his shoulders and his spirit, in the applause from her friends which felt like family, in the kiss of the man she loved.

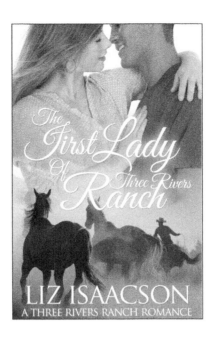

The First Lady of Three Rivers Ranch: A Three Rivers Ranch Romance (Book 8): Heidi Duffin has been dreaming about opening her own bakery since she was thirteen years old. She scrimped and saved for years to afford baking and pastry school in San Francisco. And now she only has one year left before she's a certified pastry chef. Frank Ackerman's father has recently retired, and he's taken over the largest cattle ranch in the Texas Panhandle. A horseman through and through, he's also nearing thirty-one and looking for someone to bring love and joy to a homestead that's been dominated by men for a decade. But when he convinces Heidi to come clean the cowboy cabins, she changes all that. But the siren's call of a bakery is still loud in Heidi's ears, even if she's also seeing a future with Frank. Can she rely on her faith in ways she's never had to before or will their relationship end when summer does?

SNEAK PEEK! CHAPTER ONE OF THE FIRST LADY OF THREE RIVERS RANCH

The possibilities had never been so wide open for Heidi Duffin. Though she needed a job—and quickly—she had four applications out, only one year remaining until she earned her Bachelor's degree in Baking and Pastry Arts, and a whole summer to enjoy herself.

"Why are we driving out here again?" Heidi peered into the nothingness surrounding her as her younger sister aimed their truck east down the middle of the two-lane highway.

"It's the first dance of summer in Three Rivers," Maggie said. "And Chase will be there."

Heidi frowned, her mind whirring to try to remember who Chase was. She couldn't. "And he's...?"

"He's the boy I met a couple of weeks ago in Daddy's store." Maggie glanced at Heidi, her fingers flexing on the steering wheel. "The cowboy?"

Realization lit up Heidi's mind at the same time her frown deepened. "Oh, yes. The cowboy."

"You don't have to say it like that." Maggie made her chuckle sound light, but Heidi knew annoyance sat just below the surface.

"We aren't all big city girls." Maggie lifted her chin and pressed a bit harder on the accelerator. "I like cowboys."

"And apparently driving an hour for a dance." Heidi brushed something invisible from her skirt. "He must be something special."

Maggie giggled, and Heidi was reminded of the three-year difference in their ages. "He is. You meet anyone in San Francisco?"

Heidi had been grilled by her mother, and her grandmother, and then each of her mother's three sisters. As if she needed to find a handsome chef before she finished her own journey through culinary school. As if that was the only way to have value as a woman, even though it was nineteen-eighty-six and lots of women were joining the workforce these days.

And there had been Westin....

She shook her head, dislodging the dark eyes that always seemed so angry, and said, "No, I'm too busy baking to be dating."

"Oh, come on, Heidi. Surely you don't bake all day and all night."

She sighed. "No, but some days it feels like it." And she wouldn't have it any other way, despite the aching back and sore feet. Heidi was destined to have her own bakery someday, and she would. She absolutely would. She'd thought of little else for the past two years as she went to school in San Francisco, little else for the four years it had taken her to work and save for culinary school, little else since she was thirteen years old.

"So tell me about Chase," she said to get the questions away from her.

"He's a wrangler at the Three Rivers Ranch, and he is *soo* cute," Maggie singsonged. Heidi smiled at the exuberance of her sister. Of the three she had, Maggie was Heidi's favorite. The next youngest, Bridgette, had just graduated from high school and had started cosmetology school a week ago.

The baby of the family, Kayla, still had a couple years of high school left. Heidi loved all her sisters, but she and Maggie had been through the most together, caused the most trouble, and though they were practically opposites, Heidi got along great with her. Plus, Maggie had always helped out the most when their mom had to teach piano lessons late.

The two girls had put dinner on the table every Monday, Tuesday, and Wednesday night, and sometimes more if Momma went to help Daddy at the store. He owned and operated a farming supply store, which made it possible for Maggie to meet boys like Chase.

If their daddy knew that, though...he might close his doors. Heidi let the smile she felt show on her face. She loved her parents, and they'd worked hard to provide a good life for her and her sisters. Though she'd saved and scrimped, her parents had helped pay for pastry school. And heaven knew that wasn't cheap.

Thank you, she sent heavenward, the way she had everyday for the past two years. Gratitude filled her as signs of a town finally came into view.

"Oh, thank goodness," she said, picking at her pink mini-skirt again. "I thought we'd never get here."

"It's not that far," Maggie said as she slowed and entered the town of Three Rivers. "The dance is in the park." She leaned forward as if the giant windshield didn't provide an adequate view of her destination.

She turned here and there, and the streets became choked with cars and trucks. "Is the whole town coming to this dance?" Heidi peered out her window.

"Probably," Maggie said. "Chase said it was a big deal—the first dance of the summer, Heidi!"

"Yeah, first dance."

"Chase said the only event that's bigger is the Fourth of July celebration. Rodeos, picnics, parades. He says he's gonna come pick me up for that."

"Great," Heidi deadpanned. "You already got the weekend off?"

"No," Maggie said airily. "But Bridgette will cover for me if I need her to."

"Bridgette just started school," Heidi reminded her. "She hasn't been home before ten o'clock in the past week."

Something akin to panic raced across Maggie's face. "Kayla, then."

"You haven't told Daddy about Chase, have you?"

Maggie pulled behind another truck, the park nowhere in sight. "We'll have to walk."

"Maggie," Heidi warned.

"No," she said. "Okay? No, I haven't told Momma or Daddy about Chase."

"Where do they think we are?"

"Oh, I told them we were coming out to the dance here in Three Rivers." She slid Heidi a mischievous grin that usually led to them being up a creek without a paddle. Literally, that had happened once after a cocked eyebrow like the one Maggie wore now. "I just didn't say why."

Heidi didn't want to grin at her sister, but she did, feeling younger than she had in a long time. "Okay, well, I can't wait to meet Chase."

Terror tamped out the excitement in Maggie's face. "Surely you'll find someone to dance with."

Heidi stared at her sister. "What do you mean? I came with you."

"I don't want you to meet Chase," Maggie blurted. "He'll like you more than me."

Heidi blinked, blinked. "What?"

Maggie's eyes rounded and she fiddled her fingers around each other. "You're prettier than me. And the boys always like you more."

Heidi burst into laughter, her sister's worry ridiculous. "That only happened once, and only because Elliot was a senior and was embarrassed to admit he liked a freshman."

It was Maggie's turn to blink and say, "What?"

"Yeah, that's what he told me at prom. That he really wanted to ask you, but you were too young." Heidi tossed a dry look to Maggie. "It wasn't my best date." She climbed out of the truck and took a deep breath of the fresh air. She'd give Three Rivers a nod for that. "So don't worry, Mags. I won't steal Chase from you."

They walked the two blocks to the park, where the country music could be heard after the first block. Maggie swept the crowd, looking for the one face she knew, while Heidi hung behind her. She didn't know anyone here, and she didn't really care to.

"Maggie!" a man called, and both Heidi and Maggie swung in the direction it came from. A blond cowboy pushed through the crowd and swept a giggling Maggie off her feet. His blue eyes sparkled with laughter and he slung his arm around her shoulders as they faced Heidi.

"Chase, this is my sister," Maggie said, an edge of anxiety riding in her eyes. "Heidi."

"Nice to meet you, Miss Heidi." Chase grinned and extended his hand toward Heidi. She shook it, and shuffled her feet as he turned back to Maggie and started talking.

"I'll see you later, okay?"

Heidi yanked her gaze back to Maggie. "Later?"

"Yeah, I'm gonna go dance with Chase." She squealed and spun, leaving Heidi alone in this completely foreign place. Though, for a small town, this dance was impressive. She wandered along the edges of the dance floor until she ran into the refreshment table.

"Love your skirt," a girl said, a genuine smile on her face.

"Thanks," Heidi said as she plucked a cup of red punch off the table.

"Where'd you get it?"

"San Francisco." Heidi took a sip of punch, wishing her voice didn't carry a note of pride. She wasn't better than this girl, despite her fashionable mini-skirt and oversized top with a teal stripe along the neckline.

"Do you live there?" the girl asked. "Oh, I'm Farrah."

"Nice to meet you." Heidi smiled at her. "No, I don't live there. I'm going to school there."

Farrah got a faraway look on her face. "I wish I could go to school."

A pang of sadness hit Heidi, along with a wave of gratitude and the memories of her own longing to attend school. She'd worked for her father for four long years, living at home and spending nothing, until she could pay for the first year of culinary school.

"I'm sorry," she murmured, wanting to escape from this conversation. Though the sun had started to set, it suddenly felt too hot to Heidi. "Excuse me."

She turned, and everything seemed to happen in slow motion. Someone bumped her elbow—or maybe she bumped them. No matter what, her punch went flying, the red liquid practically leaping from the cup and flying through the air.

It hit the man who'd just stepped out of the crowd, and time rushed forward again. Heidi gasped at the same time the punch touched the man. He flinched like she'd physically touched him, and glanced down at his now-stained shirt.

His now-stained *white* shirt.

Heidi brought both hands to cover her mouth, absolutely horrified. "I'm so sorry," she said through her fingers. "I got hit, and—"

"It's okay," he said, his voice low and deep and wonderful and flowing like honey over Heidi's frayed nerves. The music faded into silence; the world narrowed to just the two of them.

She slid her eyes from his shirt and up his thick chest, taking in muscular arms under his short sleeves, and over the most handsome face she'd ever seen. He had a shock of dark hair poking out from beneath a black cowboy hat, and bright, electric blue eyes that drew her in like a magnet. He looked like he hadn't shaved in a couple of days, and the facial hair added to his allure.

His belt buckle could've served as a dinner plate, and at the bottom of his long, jean-clad legs, he wore a weathered pair of cowboy boots.

Heidi forgot her own name. She swallowed and dropped her hands back to her sides. All her mind could conjure was, *Maybe cowboys aren't so bad.*

"I don't think we've met." The man moved forward a step and reached for her. No, past her, to the refreshment table, where he collected a napkin and starting dabbing at his ruined shirt. "I'm Frank Ackerman."

Heidi startled and cleared her throat. "Heidi Duffin."

"You new in town, Heidi?" He settled his weight away from her, but his near proximity rendered her weak. He smelled like leather and pine and wood and everything manly and nice.

She took a deep breath of him, wanting to bake him into a pie so the aroma would infect the air for a long time. "Yes. I mean, no." She took a step back to give herself some air. "No, I don't live here. I'm just here with my sister." She scanned the crowd, half-hoping Maggie would appear to corroborate her story. "I guess she's dating some guy from some ranch—"

"Three Rivers Ranch?"

"Yeah, that's it." Heidi found his face again and smiled at him. When he returned the gesture, she thought sure she'd faint. She wondered if he knew how handsome he was, how fast her heart was racing, how he affected girls. "Anyway, I'm from Amarillo," she finished.

"You wanna dance?" He nodded his hat toward the dance floor.

Heidi hadn't intended to dance with anyone. Her brain screamed at her to say no. Her heart reminded her how she felt about cowboys, about living so far from civilization, about belt buckles the size of hubcaps.

But her voice said, "Sure," and a thrill of excitement tripped down her spine when Frank put his warm hand on the small of her back and guided her through the crowd.

FRANK DIDN'T KNOW THE PRETTY LITTLE WOMAN WHO'D SPLASHED punch down his chest, but he wanted to. Heidi had a calming voice, and though his shirt was starting to stick to his skin, he couldn't risk leaving her to clean up before he had a chance to dance with her. Someone else would pounce on a pretty woman like her.

She sported light brown hair the color of the river rocks out at Frank's ranch. Well, not really *his* ranch. At least not yet. As the eldest of three brothers, the ranch was being passed to him at the end of the year. He'd been knee-deep in figuring out how to run a twenty thousand acre cattle ranch without the help of his father.

Frank wanted the ranch, always had. That wasn't the problem. But he also wanted someone to run it with, and therein sat the biggest problem of Frank's life. His mother had died a decade ago, and Frank had seen how a ranch as vast and busy as Three Rivers could swallow a man. He'd watched his father disappear behind the desk, vanish out on the range, become a ghost in his own house.

Frank didn't want to be like his father. He wanted his life to be as vibrant as the ranch itself, full of laughter and family and food. And to do that, he needed a good woman who could introduce that spirit the way his mom had.

He'd been trying to find her for the past six months. Of course, he hadn't told any of the women he'd dated that, but he'd never made it that far in his relationships. He kept that desire close to the vest, worried it might scare a woman away.

As Heidi turned and slipped herself easily into his arms, he couldn't help picturing her out at Three Rivers. The thought brought a smile to his lips, and he gazed down into her more-brown-than-hazel eyes and found strength there.

"So what do you do in Amarillo?" he asked as the band started a mid-tempo tune he could twirl and hold Heidi to.

"Oh, I don't really live in Amarillo."

"No?"

"Well, I do, but I don't." She giggled, but quickly smothered it.

"Well, that makes all kinds of sense," he teased.

"My family lives there. I'm just home for the summer. I'm going to school in San Francisco."

Frank's heart dipped down to his boots, where it stayed for a few beats before rebounding to his chest. "What're you studying?"

"Baking and pastry arts." She practically glowed, and Frank itched to run his fingers down the side of her face. "I'm going to open a bakery after I graduate."

So she could cook. Frank liked a woman who knew her way around a kitchen. "That's great," he said, genuine about her baking, but not liking that she wouldn't be around very long. "What are you doin' this summer?"

"Trying to find a job." She possessed a quiet power, which called to Frank's soul.

"I can help with that," he said.

"Oh?" She gazed up at him with an open expression, her petite hand pressing into his shoulder warm and welcome.

"Sure," he said. "I heard Three Rivers Ranch needs someone to clean their cowboy cabins this summer."

She blinked, distracting him with her long lashes. "I'm sure that won't work."

"Why not?" Frank pulled his gaze from her and looked around as if he didn't mind if she turned him down. But he did. He wanted to see her everyday, get to know her better, and he couldn't drive to Amarillo at the drop of a hat. Or even once a week.

"Because I live in Amarillo." Her fingers inched down his arm, and Frank's stomach flipped.

"You could live on the ranch." What was he saying? He felt as if he was grasping for straws.

A beautiful blush stained her cheeks. "Do you live on the ranch, Mister Ackerman?"

He met her eye again, pleased by the ring of desire he saw there. "Well...." He didn't want to tell her he actually owned the ranch. Or that he would in six months when his father signed everything over to him and made it official. He'd kept that information private for as long as possible too. Seemed once women discovered that he was about to become the owner of the ranch, they were doubly interested.

Sure, the ranch was profitable. Some would say he was rich. But he didn't want the ranch to be the reason someone liked him, and that had been happening more and more lately.

"Well, what?" Heidi pressed.

"Yeah, I live on the ranch."

"And you just happen to know that I could live out there and clean cabins?"

"Yes."

She cocked her head to the side, a cute gesture that only made Frank more interested in Heidi Duffin. "I'll think about it."

Which meant no. The song neared its end, and Frank felt frantic. She'd step away, melt into the crowd, and he'd never see her again. He wasn't sure what to do, and he offered a desperate prayer for help.

What do I say?

Nothing came to mind. The song ended, and sure enough, Heidi fell back. "Thank you for the dance, Mister Ackerman."

"Wait," he blurted as she started to turn. His eyes slid down her clothes, landing on her black sandals before bouncing back to her face. He couldn't just let her walk out of his life. "I need to get your phone number."

Her eyebrows shot toward her hairline. "You do?"

Thinking fast, he gestured to his ruined shirt. "Yeah. I'll need to send you a cleaning bill."

Horror washed over her face, and Frank immediately regretted his tactic to get her phone number. He just knew he couldn't let her walk away. He moved closer as another song started up, this one much louder and faster than the previous tune.

"Of course, if you let me take you down the street to the ice cream parlor, I could forget about the ruined shirt." He grinned at her, well aware of the power of his straight, white teeth and flirtatious tone.

She seemed as susceptible to his smile as most other women, a curve playing with her pink lips. Frank cleared his throat, aware he'd leaned closer and closer to her. Heidi looped her arm through his. "I love mint chocolate chip. Do they have that?"

He'd personally make her some if they didn't. "I'm sure they do." He led her off the dance floor, relief rushing through him with the force of river rapids. "I'm more of a praline and caramel kind of man myself."

"That's my daddy's favorite flavor," she said.

"He must be an amazing man, then."

Heidi practically wilted beside him, and Frank wondered if he'd struck gold by going to the dance tonight. He hadn't planned on coming. Didn't even want to. His cowhands would attend all summer long, but as the boss, Frank rarely went with them. Plus, his age set him apart from the crowd. And his status, his last attempt at a girlfriend had told him.

After Whitney had said every girl watched him wherever he went, he'd stayed out at Three Rivers, only coming to town for church. He'd even been sending a cowhand—and paying him —to do his grocery shopping. Lots of women at the grocery store, and Frank didn't need them ogling him while he was trying to select the right variety of apple. Or hitting on him while he put milk in his cart. Or gossiping about when the thirty-year-old bachelor would find a wife and take over the ranch.

"Frank?"

"Hmm?" He returned to the warm evening, the weight of Heidi's fingers on his arm.

"I asked what you do for a living."

"Oh, uh." Frank's feet dragged against the cement. He didn't want to lie, but he didn't want to tell her either. "I'm out at the ranch." Not really a fib, if God didn't count omission as a lie.

"Oh, that's right. You like it? The life of a wrangler?"

"Yeah, it's great." Frank reached for the door handle and pulled. The bell on the ice cream parlor's door jingled and a woman lifted her head.

"Hey, Frank," she said with an obvious note of suggestion in her voice. Frank cursed himself for coming in, for not remembering that Victoria worked at the shop. They'd gone out a few times, right at the beginning of Frank's dating spree, and while Vickie was easy on the eyes, that was where her beauty ended.

"Evenin', Vickie." Frank tightened his arm against his side, keeping Heidi right next to him.

"Here for the flavor of the month?" Vickie's appraising gaze slid over Heidi. "Oh, it looks like you already found one."

Heat flamed in Frank's face. He hadn't intentionally tried to speed through several women in Three Rivers, but unfortunately he didn't need very many dates to decide if he liked someone or not.

Heidi's hand slipped out of his arm, and she put several steps between them as she moved up to the counter. "Do you have mint chocolate chip?" Her voice sounded on the upper range of her octave, though Frank had just met her and didn't know for certain.

"Yes." Vickie scooped with extra vigor while Frank glared, hoping she could feel the weight and displeasure in his gaze.

———

THE NEXT MORNING, FRANK STRODE FROM THE HOMESTEAD through the yard to the cowboy cabins. He counted down six to Chase's, climbed the steps, and knocked on the door. Several seconds passed before the blond cowboy opened the door.

"Boss," he said, falling back a step in obvious surprise. "Come in." He swiped a cowboy hat from a hook on the wall and smashed it on his bedhead. "What brings you here this mornin'?" Chase yawned as he backed into the kitchen. "Coffee?"

Frank waved him away. "No, I'm fine, Chase." He glanced around the cabin, the questions he had obvious and embarrassing.

Chase busied himself making coffee anyway, and Frank realized he'd woken the cowboy on his only morning off this week. "Chase," he said. "I'm sorry. I just realized I woke you."

"It's fine." Chase tossed a smile over his shoulder. "I'm up now."

"I'll give you Monday morning off too."

Chase's grin widened. "Really?"

"Really."

"Great." He finished with the coffee and faced Frank. "So, what can I do for you?"

Frank cleared his throat. He'd always been able to just say what needed to be said. It was one of his greatest strengths. "The girl you met at the dance last night, what was her name?"

Chase's eyes narrowed. "Maggie."

"Maggie, right." Frank remembered that Heidi had said she had three sisters. "And she has sisters?"

"Yeah." Chase drew the word out, waiting, extreme curiosity burning through his eyes.

Frank dropped his gaze to his cowboy boots. "You have her phone number?" He'd left Heidi on the outskirts of the dance after they'd licked their cones gone and walked the perimeter of the park twice. He'd wanted to hold her hand while they walked, hug her good-bye, ask for her phone number himself, but Vickie's poisoned words had caused Heidi to put distance between them. She hadn't touched him again, a fact every cell in Frank's body had been mourning for the past ten hours.

"You want to call my girl?" The incredulity in Chase's voice hit Frank like a punch.

"No," he said quickly, lifting his eyes to his cowhand's. "No, of course not. Her sister. Maggie came to the dance last night with her sister, Heidi. I want to call her, but I wasn't able to get her number before they left."

Realization and relief sagged Chase's bunched shoulders. A knowing smile followed. "I saw you two dancing. She's pretty."

Frank wasn't interested in gossiping about Heidi's beauty. "So can I have the number?"

Chase got up and retrieved a slip of paper from his messy kitchen counter. "What are you gonna do? Just call her and...then what? What will you tell her about how you got her number?"

Frank didn't know, and he admitted as much to Chase. "Any ideas?" he asked.

"Maybe she won't ask," Chase said.

Frank knew she would. He didn't know everything about Heidi Duffin, but he'd seen the sharpness in her eyes, enjoyed the wit in their conversation, and he knew she was smart. "She'll ask," he said, his heart plummeting though Chase handed him the paper with the number written on it. "Maybe I'll just see if she applies for the housekeeping job."

But he knew she wouldn't. She'd made her position clear about living out at the ranch, calling Three Rivers "the middle of nowhere," and asking him if he liked living so far from the city.

She seemed his opposite in every way, and yet he'd barely

been able to sleep for want of seeing her again, hearing her voice, answering her questions, learning all he could about her. He mashed the paper in his fist and stuffed it in his pocket. "Thanks, Chase."

"You'll think of something," Chase called as Frank opened the door and left the cabin. "Let me know how it goes!"

But Frank wouldn't. Because he wasn't going to call Heidi Duffin and tell her he'd gone crawling to her sister's boyfriend to get her phone number. A phone number she hadn't chosen to give him.

Read THE FIRST LADY OF THREE RIVERS RANCH now!

READ MORE BY LIZ ISAACSON

Love Three Rivers Ranch and want to stay here? Perfect! Go back in time and see how the ranch got it's heritage in THE FIRST LADY OF THREE RIVERS RANCH.

Interested in more rodeo romance? Read about Tanner Wolf in Lucky Number Thirteen, Book 10 in the Three Rivers Ranch Romance series.

Ready to journey to another ranch filled with former rodeo stars who now train horses for the circuit? Go to Brush Creek, Utah, and start the Brush Creek Brides Romance series with A WEDDING FOR THE WIDOWER.

BOOKS IN THE THREE RIVERS RANCH ROMANCE SERIES:

Second Chance Ranch: A Three Rivers Ranch Romance (Book 1): After his deployment, injured and discharged Major Squire Ackerman returns to Three Rivers Ranch, wanting to forgive Kelly for ignoring him a decade ago. He'd like to provide the stable life she needs, but with old wounds opening and a ranch on the brink of financial collapse, it will take patience and faith to make their second chance possible.

**Third Time's the Charm: A Three Rivers Ranch Romance
(Book 2):** First Lieutenant Peter Marshall has a truckload of debt
and no way to provide for a family, but Chelsea helps him see
past all the obstacles, all the scars. With so many unknowns, can
Pete and Chelsea develop the love, acceptance, and faith needed
to find their happily ever after?

Fourth and Long: A Three Rivers Ranch Romance (Book 3): Commander Brett Murphy goes to Three Rivers Ranch to find some rest and relaxation with his Army buddies. Having his ex-wife show up with a seven-year-old she claims is his son is anything but the R&R he craves. Kate needs to make amends, and Brett needs to find forgiveness, but are they too late to find their happily ever after?

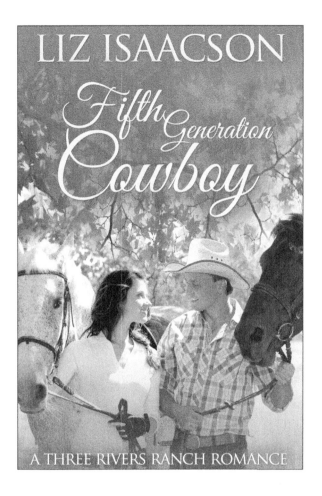

Fifth Generation Cowboy: A Three Rivers Ranch Romance (Book 4): Tom Lovell has watched his friends find their true happiness on Three Rivers Ranch, but everywhere he looks, he only sees friends. Rose Reyes has been bringing her daughter out to the ranch for equine therapy for months, but it doesn't seem to be working. Her challenges with Mari are just as frustrating as ever. Could Tom be exactly what Rose needs? Can he remove his friendship blinders and find love with someone who's been right in front of him all this time?

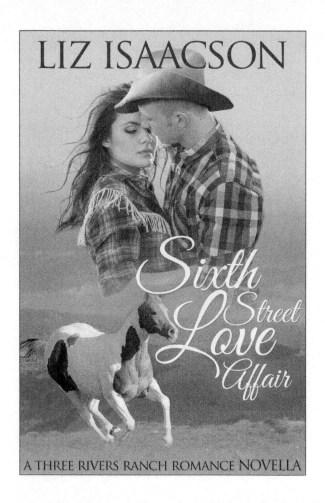

LIZ ISAACSON

Sixth Street Love Affair

A THREE RIVERS RANCH ROMANCE NOVELLA

Sixth Street Love Affair: A Three Rivers Ranch Romance (Book 5): After losing his wife a few years back, Garth Ahlstrom thinks he's ready for a second chance at love. But Juliette Thompson has a secret that could destroy their budding relationship. Can they find the strength, patience, and faith to make things work?

The Seventh Sergeant: A Three Rivers Ranch Romance (Book 6): Life has finally started to settle down for Sergeant Reese Sanders after his devastating injury overseas. Discharged from the Army and now with a good job at Courage Reins, he's finally found happiness—until a horrific fall puts him right back where he was years ago: Injured and depressed. Carly Watters, Reese's new veteran care coordinator, dislikes small towns almost as much as she loathes cowboys. But she finds herself faced with both when she gets assigned to Reese's case. Do they have the humility and faith to make their relationship more than professional?

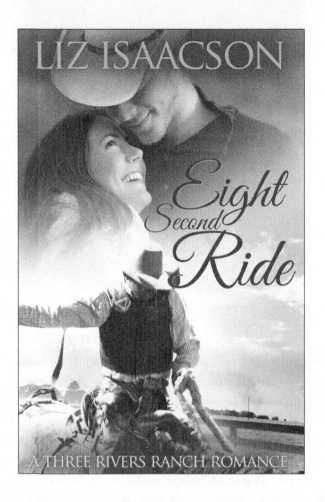

Eight Second Ride: A Three Rivers Ranch Romance (Book 7): Ethan Greene loves his work at Three Rivers Ranch, but he can't seem to find the right woman to settle down with. When sassy yet vulnerable Brynn Bowman shows up at the ranch to recruit him back to the rodeo circuit, he takes a different approach with the barrel racing champion. His patience and newfound faith pay off when a friendship--and more--starts with Brynn. But she wants out of the rodeo circuit right when Ethan wants to rejoin. Can they find the path God wants them to take and still stay together?

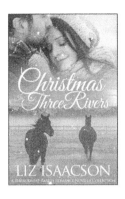

Christmas in Three Rivers: A Three Rivers Ranch Romance (Book 9): Isn't Christmas the best time to fall in love? The cowboys of Three Rivers Ranch think so. Join four of them as they journey toward their path to happily ever after in four, all-new novellas in the Amazon #1 Bestselling Three Rivers Ranch Romance series.

THE NINTH INNING: The Christmas season has never felt like such a burden to boutique owner Andrea Larsen. But with Mama gone and the holidays upon her, Andy finds herself wishing she hadn't been so quick to judge her former boyfriend, cowboy Lawrence Collins. Well, Lawrence hasn't forgotten about Andy either, and he devises a plan to get her out to the ranch so they can reconnect. Do they have the faith and humility to patch things up and start a new relationship?

TEN DAYS IN TOWN: Sandy Keller is tired of the dating scene in Three Rivers. Though she owns the pancake house, she's looking for a fresh start, which means an escape from the town where she grew up. When her older brother's best friend, Tad Jorgensen, comes to town for the holidays, it is a balm to his weary soul. A helicopter tour guide who experienced a near-death experience, he's looking to start over too--but in Three Rivers. Can Sandy and Tad navigate their troubles to find the path God wants them to take--and discover true love--in only ten days?

ELEVEN YEAR REUNION: Pastry chef extraordinaire, Grace

Lewis has moved to Three Rivers to help Heidi Ackerman open a bakery in Three Rivers. Grace relishes the idea of starting over in a town where no one knows about her failed cupcakery. She doesn't expect to run into her old high school boyfriend, Jonathan Carver. A carpenter working at Three Rivers Ranch, Jon's in town against his will. But with Grace now on the scene, Jon's thinking life in Three Rivers is suddenly looking up. But with her focus on baking and his disdain for small towns, can they make their eleven year reunion stick?

THE TWELFTH TOWN: Newscaster Taryn Tucker has had enough of life on-screen. She's bounced from town to town before arriving in Three Rivers, completely alone and completely anonymous--just the way she now likes it. She takes a job cleaning at Three Rivers Ranch, hoping for a chance to figure out who she is and where God wants her. When she meets happy-go-lucky cowhand Kenny Stockton, she doesn't expect sparks to fly. Kenny's always been "the best friend" for his female friends, but the pull between him and Taryn can't be denied. Will they have the courage and faith necessary to make their opposite worlds mesh?

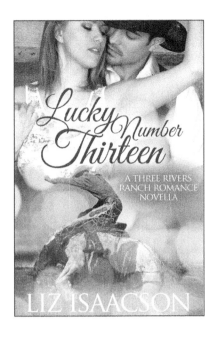

Lucky Number Thirteen: A Three Rivers Ranch Romance (Book 10): Tanner Wolf, a rodeo champion ten times over, is excited to be riding in Three Rivers for the first time since he left his philandering ways and found religion. Seeing his old friends Ethan and Brynn is therapuetic--until a terrible accident lands him in the hospital. With his rodeo career over, Tanner thinks maybe he'll stay in town--and it's not just because his nurse, Summer Hamblin, is the prettiest woman he's ever met. But Summer's the queen of first dates, and as she looks for a way to make a relationship with the transient rodeo star work Summer's not sure she has the fortitude to go on a second date. Can they find love among the tragedy?

BOOKS IN THE GOLD VALLEY ROMANCE SERIES:

Before the Leap: A Gold Valley Romance (Book 1): Jace Lovell only has one thing left after his fiancé abandons him at the altar: his job at Horseshoe Home Ranch. He throws himself into becoming the best foreman the ranch has ever had—and that includes hiring an interior designer to make the ranch owner's wife happy. Belle Edmunds is back in Gold Valley and she's desperate to build a portfolio that she can use to start her own firm in Montana. She applies for the job at Horseshoe Home, and though Jace and Belle grew up together, they've never seen eye to eye on much more than the sky is blue. Jace isn't anywhere near forgiving his fiancé, and he's not sure he's ready for a new relationship with someone as fiery and beautiful as Belle. Can she employ her patience while he figures out how to forgive so they can find their own brand of happily-ever-after?

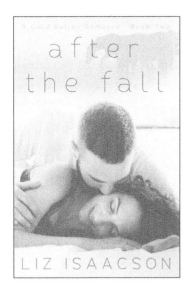

After the Fall: A Gold Valley Romance (Book 2): Professional snowboarder Sterling Maughan has sequestered himself in his family's cabin in the exclusive mountain community above Gold Valley, Montana after a devastating fall that ended his career. Lost, with no direction and no motivation, the last thing he wants is company. But Norah Watson has other plans for the cabin. Not only does she clean Sterling's cabin, she's a counselor at Silver Creek, a teen rehabilitation center at the base of the mountain that uses horses to aid in the rebuilding of lives, and she brings her girls up to the cabin every twelve weeks. When Sterling finds out there's a job for an at-risk counselor at Silver Creek, he asks Norah to drive him back and forth. He learns to ride horses and use equine therapy to help his boys—and himself. The more time they spend together, the more convinced Norah is to never tell Sterling about her troubled past, let him see her house on the wrong side of the tracks, or meet her mother. But Sterling is interested in all things Norah, and as his body heals, so does his faith. Will Norah be able to trust Sterling so they can have a chance at true love?

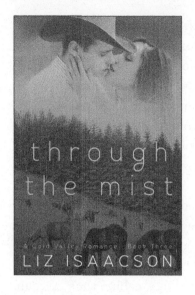

Through the Mist: A Gold Valley Romance (Book 3): Landon Edmunds has been a cowboy his whole life. An accident five years ago ended his successful rodeo career, and now he's looking to start a horse ranch of his own, and he's looking outside of Montana. Which would be great if God hadn't brought Megan Palmer back to Gold Valley right when Landon is looking to leave. As the preacher's daughter, Megan isn't that excited to be back in her childhood hometown. Megan and Landon work together well, and as sparks fly, she's sure God brought her back to Gold Valley so she could find her happily ever after. Through serious discussion and prayer, can Landon and Megan find their future together?

Be sure to check out the spinoff series, the Brush Creek Brides romances after you read THROUGH THE MIST. Start with A WEDDING FOR THE WIDOWER.

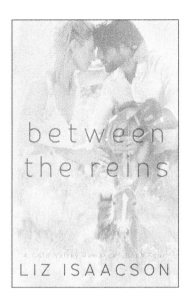

Between the Reins: A Gold Valley Romance (Book 4): Twelve years ago, Owen Carr left Gold Valley—and his longtime girlfriend—in favor of a country music career in Nashville. Married and divorced, Natalie teaches ballet at the dance studio in Gold Valley, but she never auditioned for the professional company the way she dreamed of doing. With Owen back, she realizes all the opportunities she missed out on when he left all those years ago —including a future with him. Can they mend broken bridges in order to have a second chance at love?

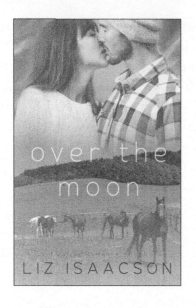

Over the Moon: A Gold Valley Romance (Book 5): Holly Gray is back in Gold Valley after her failed engagement five years ago. She just needs her internship hours on the ranch so she can finish her veterinarian degree and return to Vermont. She wasn't planning on rekindling many friendships, and she certainly wasn't planning on running into a familiar face at Horseshoe Home Ranch. But it's not the face she was dreading seeing—it's his twin brother, Caleb Chamberlain. Caleb knows Holly was his twin's fiancé at one point, but he can't deny the sparks between them. Can they navigate a rocky and secret past to find a future together?

Journey to Steeple Ridge Farm with Holly — and fall in love with the cowboys there in the Steeple Ridge Romance series! Start with STARTING OVER AT STEEPLE RIDGE.

Under the Bridge: A Gold Valley Romance (Book 6): Ty Barker has been dancing through the last thirty years of his life--and he's suddenly realized he's alone. River Lee Whitely is back in Gold Valley with her two little girls after a divorce that's left deep scars. She has a job at Silver Creek that requires her to be able to ride a horse, and she nearly tramples Ty at her first lesson. That's just fine by him, because River Lee is the girl Ty has never gotten over.

Ty realizes River Lee needs time to settle into her new job, her new home, her new life as a single parent, but going slow has never been his style. But for River Lee, can Ty take the necessary steps to keep her in his life?

Up on the Housetop: A Gold Valley Romance (Book 7): Archer Bailey has already lost one job to Emersyn Enders, so he deliberately doesn't tell her about the cowhand job up at Horseshoe Home Ranch. Emery's temporary job is ending, but her obligations to her physically disabled sister aren't. As Archer and Emery work together, its clear that the sparks flying between them aren't all from their friendly competition over a job. Will Emery and Archer be able to navigate the ranch, their close quarters, and their individual circumstances to find love this holiday season?

BOOKS IN THE BRUSH CREEK BRIDES ROMANCE SERIES:

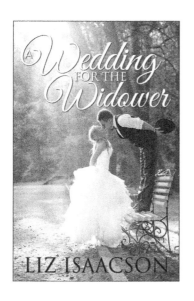

A Wedding for the Widower: Brush Creek Brides Romance (Book 1): Former rodeo champion and cowboy Walker Thompson trains horses at Brush Creek Horse Ranch, where he lives a simple life in his cabin with his ten-year-old son. A widower of six years, he's worked with Tess Wagner, a widow who came to Brush Creek to escape the turmoil of her life to give her seven-year-old son a slower pace of life. But Tess's breast cancer is back...

Walker will have to decide if he'd rather spend even a short time with Tess than not have her in his life at all. Tess wants to feel God's love and power, but can she discover and accept God's will in order to find her happy ending?

A Companion for the Cowboy: Brush Creek Brides Romance (Book 2): Cowboy and professional roper Justin Jackman has found solitude at Brush Creek Horse Ranch, preferring his time with the animals he trains over dating. With two failed engagements in his past, he's not really interested in getting his heart stomped on again. But when flirty and fun Renee Martin picks him up at a church ice cream bar--on a bet, no less-- he finds himself more than just

a little interested. His Gen-X attitudes are attractive to her; her Millennial behaviors drive him nuts. Can Justin look past their differences and take a chance on another engagement?

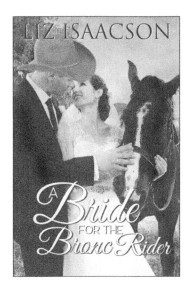

A Bride for the Bronc Rider: Brush Creek Brides Romance (Book 3): Ted Caldwell has been a retired bronc rider for years, and he thought he was perfectly happy training horses to buck at Brush Creek Ranch. He was wrong. When he meets April Nox, who comes to the ranch to hide her pregnancy from all her friends back in Jackson Hole, Ted realizes he has a huge family-shaped hole in his life. April is embarrassed, heartbroken, and trying to find her extinguished faith. She's never ridden a horse and wants nothing to do with a cowboy ever again. Can Ted and April create a family of happiness and love from a tragedy?

A Family for the Farmer: Brush Creek Brides Romance (Book 4): Blake Gibbons oversees all the agriculture at Brush Creek Horse Ranch, sometimes moonlighting as a general contractor. When he meets Erin Shields, new in town, at her aunt's bakery, he's instantly smitten. Erin moved to Brush Creek after a divorce that left her penniless, homeless, and a single mother of three children under age eight. She's nowhere near ready to start dating again, but the

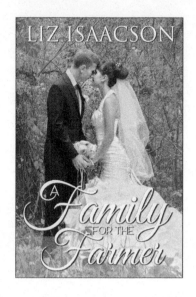

longer Blake hangs around the bakery, the more she starts to like him. Can Blake and Erin find a way to blend their lifestyles and become a family?

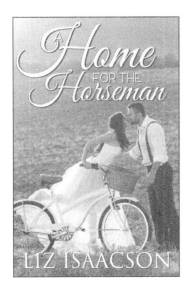

A Home for the Horseman: Brush Creek Brides Romance (Book 5): Emmett Graves has always had a positive outlook on life. He adores training horses to become barrel racing champions during the day and cuddling with his cat at night. Fresh off her professional rodeo retirement, Molly Brady comes to Brush Creek Horse Ranch as Emmett's protege. He's not thrilled, and she's allergic to cats. Oh, and she'd like to stay cowboy-free, thank you very much. But Emmett's about as cowboy as they come.... Can Emmett and Molly work together without falling in love?

A Refuge for the Rancher: Brush Creek Brides Romance (Book 6): Grant Ford spends his days training cattle—when he's not camped out at the elementary school hoping to catch a glimpse of his ex-girlfriend. When principal Shannon Sharpe confronts him and asks him to stay away from the school, the spark between them is instant and hot. Shannon's expecting a transfer very soon, but she also needs a summer outdoor coordinator—and  Grant fits the bill. Just because he's handsome and everything Shannon's ever wanted in a cowboy husband means nothing. Will Grant and Shannon be able to survive the summer or will the Utah heat be too much for them to handle?

ABOUT LIZ

Liz Isaacson writes inspirational romance, usually set in Texas, or Montana, or anywhere else horses and cowboys exist. She lives in Utah, where she teaches elementary school, taxis her daughter to dance several times a week, and eats a lot of Ferrero Rocher while writing. Find her on her website at lizisaacson.com.

Made in the USA
Monee, IL
24 August 2022